I0698913

Neon Hemlock Press
www.neonhemlock.com
@neonhemlock

© Stories copyrighted 2023-2024
© 2025 for anthology as a whole

Baffling Year Four
Edited by dave ring and Kel Coleman

Cover Design by Ocean Salazar
Cover Design by dave ring
Interior Design and Layout by dave ring

Print ISBN-13: 978-1-966503-16-3
Ebook ISBN-13: 978-1-966503-17-0

edited by dave ring and Kel Coleman
BAFFLING YEAR FOUR
Neon Hemlock Press

Baffling
Year Four

EDITED BY DAVE RING
AND KEL COLEMAN

ASSISTANT EDITOR
AUN-JULI RIDDLE

ASSOCIATE EDITORS
BENDI BARRETT, ATHAR FIKRY,
KENGO NELSON & D. A. VOROBYOV

SPECULATIVE FLASH FICTION

WITH A QUEER BENT

CONTENTS

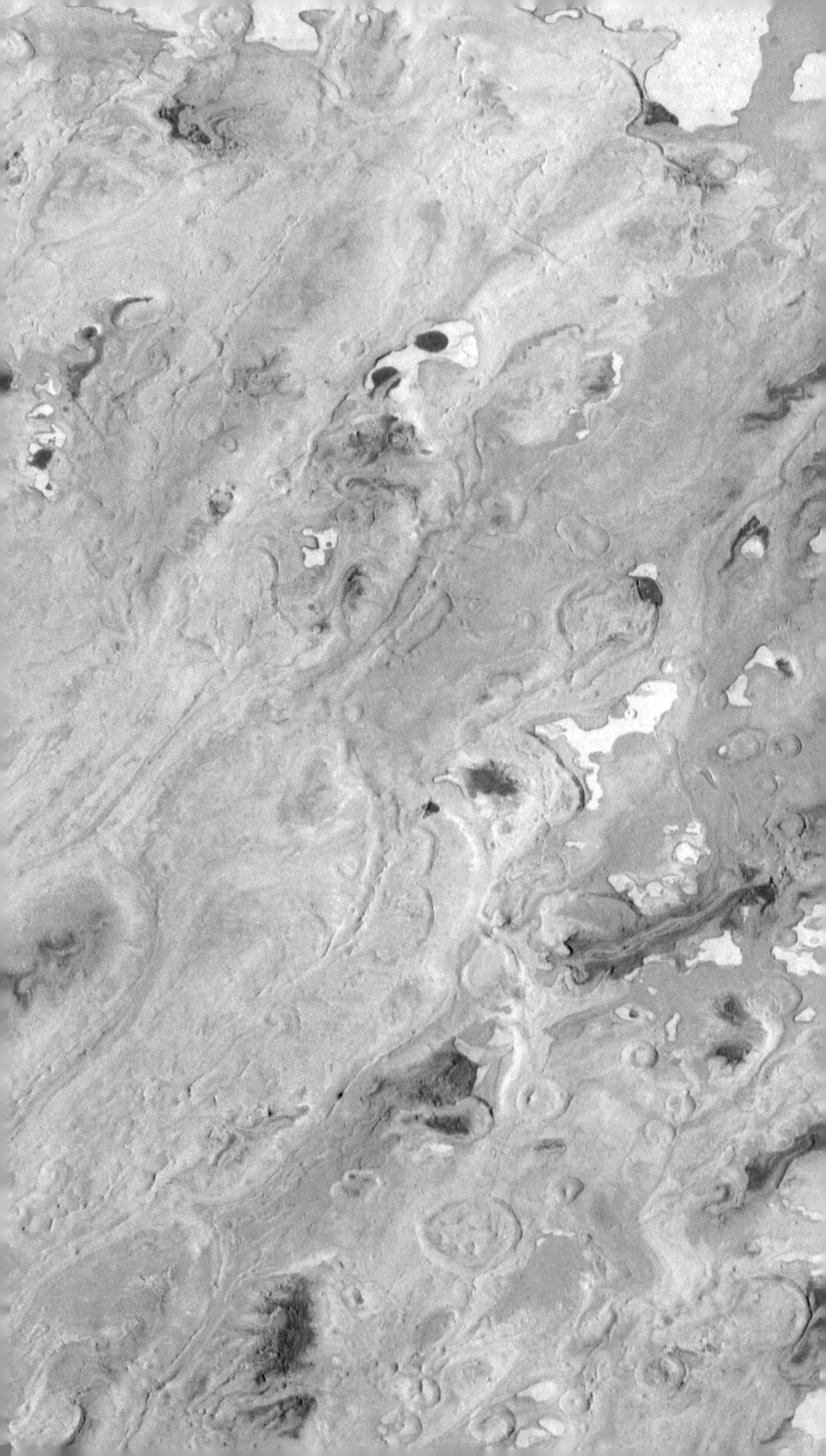

THE SUCCUBUS AND THE STORE CLERK

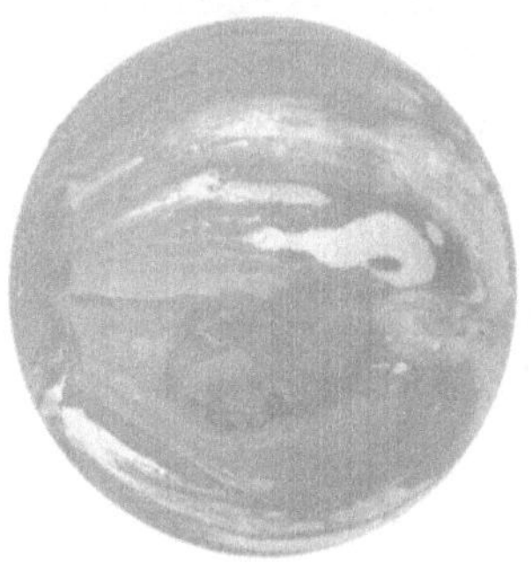

A.D. SUI

HUNGER HAS MANY faces. It's the gnawing in the stomach, yes, but it's the trembling of a hand too, the acid on the tongue, the sharp inhale of oxygen to the lungs. I guess what I'm trying to say is that I ring through Margo's cigarettes like every other day, while she taps away on the counter with freshly painted crimson nails. Every cell in my body hungers for her, and she doesn't notice it.

"Hot date?" I ask her, and she rolls her eyes.

"Where are you taking them?"

"Just to my place," Margo says and slides some change over the counter. The quarters grind against the thick plastic covering the lotto tickets. "For dinner."

We smile at our joke. But she doesn't know how jealous I am that they get to taste her lips before they die.

†

THE LITTLE LUMP inside me grows. It starts where the hunger does and spreads to every distant corner of me, chews on me, poisons me, until there is no more *me* left. Soon, *very* soon, I will give in to its appetites. On the good days, I can laugh at Margo's jokes and smoke cigarettes with her. On the bad days, I lean on the shop counter and pray for an end, empty my stomach in the plastic-lined bin. Those days, Margo brings me silks and fine perfumes in antique bottles to distract me because the sweets she once brought will only make it worse. I don't ask how long she's had them. I don't tell her they are of little help.

A convenience store is a pathetic place to die, I tell myself.

†

MARGO'S LIT WINDOW is a beacon at half past midnight. It overlooks a sprawling garden, bustling during the day, but now completely abandoned. The allure she carries with her every day pours past the open curtains. Margo's lithe silhouette moves against the ornate burgundy and gold wallpaper, one hand gliding along the zipper of her velvet dress before it pools at her ankles. There's someone else there of predictable appearence. Margo has a type. I spy from behind a rosebush as she pulls him close by the tie.

"I hope you enjoyed yourself," I say, narrating the play unfolding before me.

I say his part out loud too. "I was hoping we were only getting started." Before long, Margo kisses him. At first, he's into it, hands running up Margo's ass. As the seconds tick on by, he realizes the danger he's in, and starts to fight. But Margo is stronger, and Margo is hungry. It takes no effort at all for her to pin the squirming specimen to the wall and drain him dry. With every drop she glows more vibrant.

I wonder how it would feel to be pressed up against that wall, to inhale her scent as the life was drained from me.

†

TODAY IS A bad day. Margo sits on the windowsill, legs draped over the side. The tip of her cigarette glows orange with every inhale. "You didn't watch tonight," she says, hurt. From my bed, she's a ghostly shadow against the night, black hair rushing down naked shoulders.

Today the pain was too much, and I didn't have it in me to watch her feast. This is the first time I've missed our weekly *dinner date* since she first asked me to observe them, ten years ago. She said it elevated the flavour of her meals: a dash of acid cutting through an otherwise rich dish. "I'm sorry." The apology falls flat. Best not to draw it out. "I never asked, but what happens to them? Do they disappear into the ether once they pass your lips, or do they linger?"

"They linger." Margo takes another drag of her cigarette. "I feel them like the ocean feels every fish in its waters. They move inside me, animate me, every memory, every experience."

When I first told her of my illness, she said nothing, only summoned sweets from Paris and left them by my door. When my hair thinned and fell out in clumps, she gifted me beautiful Hermès scarves and matching silk skirts to wear. And when all my struggles were proven futile, she drank fine wines with me in silence and held my hand.

"You've never tried to take my life."

Margo laughs with the notes of antiquated crystal. "I never wanted to."

"Why not?" Better to die in bed with a succubus than alone in a convenience shop.

As if reading my mind, Margo slips into my bed beside me. Her body moves against mine like a current, flowing, beckoning. Her hands explore generously. She smells of Sunday church service and everything unholy, of roses and cemeteries and death. "I thought you liked men," I breathe into her neck.

"I like them well enough," she whispers. "But I *love* women." She whispers something else too: words, epitaphs, not for my ears, but to be etched along my flesh, like a curse, like a blessing. I can't find anything sacrilegious in the way we surrender to one another, in the way our breath meets in silent prayer.

"I'd like you to," I tell Margo when we finally rest against one another. I cannot think of a better way to spend what little life I have left, even as it leaves me breathless with exhaustion. "There's not much left, but it's yours if you want it."

She hesitates. "It's not immortality, chérie, just that your energy—"

"Will be with you for as long as you live?"

She nods. Her forehead, slick with sweat, presses against my shoulder. "I'll always know that you're there."

What is death if not satiation? What is death but a feeling where no want exists, no hunger? To rest somewhere safe—I could die for that. Margo will keep me safe, I'm sure.

"I'd like for you to do it now, if it's all the same." I'm not sure how much longer I can stay awake, and I want to fall asleep with her fingers in my hair.

Margo's cool palm cups the side of my face and turns me towards her. Her eyes are a starless sky beneath heavy eyelashes. "It'll be just like falling asleep," she whispers, and presses her lips against mine.

And she's right. Dying feels a lot like falling asleep, when you go willingly. Margo drinks my breath, and with it goes the pain and the fatigue. Another breath, and all of me rushes past her full lips. I become the air in her lungs, the blood running through her veins. I am every beat of her heart, every ache, and every longing. She savours what's left of me like the final sip of a fine wine, or the last drag of the Gauloises she brought from France two summers ago.

With her, I hunger for nothing.

WHO IS TRULY ALONE ON THE BEACH?

ANJA HENDRIKSE LIU

SHE'S NEVER ALONE, she claims. She has the waves. They devour the pebbles of the beach and run up to the crooked door of her house; with the voices of the ocean for company, she couldn't be lonely. So she says.

The townsfolk know it's untrue. All women need someone, someone to keep their feet on the earth. Even if they're monster-women, raging women, not women at all, not really, not with teeth that never smile. Not with eyes always drawn to the unfaithful ocean. Not with words that rip into things, things with no need for holes.

So they're doing her a favor, the townsfolk, the land-bound, the bold men—yes, usually men. They venture from their warm safe houses and the arms of their wives, down to the beach where the unmoored woman walks at dawn. Duty calls them to save her, as they've saved many others;

this is no place for a woman, this beach, this unprotected house, this dirty, solitary, almost-washed-away house. They'll take her somewhere secure and solid.

She's waiting when they arrive.

Unlike the ones before her who lived in this house, she's opened the crooked door, stepped out to wait ankle-deep in the surf.

But just like the ones before, she waits alone.

The rescue party sees this. They walk faster, unsheathing their thick-tendoned hands.

They should have listened.

Waves stretch to meet them, carrying the voices of those they saved in seasons past, the ones who never needed anything more than a home, who never needed saving at all. They come as foam, at first, then muscular waves, then overpowering currents that still remember the sound of fists pounding down a crooked door.

These waves know what it's like to be uprooted and dragged away from their mooring-place. Today, the townsfolk, the land-bound, will learn how it feels, too.

When the townsfolk begin to run, they're already in too deep.

She watches. Not hiding. Not alone.

Of course, she was never alone, was she?

CHANGELING

LINDSAY KING-MILLER

"**W**HEN YOU WERE a baby, you were stolen by the fairies," my mother says over dinner.

I keep eating my salad. She tells this story a lot.

"They left a baby in your crib, and she looked exactly like you. Those same blonde curls, those pink cheeks. Those sparkling hazel eyes. You were such a pretty baby." The past tense stings, as always.

I used to believe this story, when I was little. I even tried to tell some girls at school, so they'd know I was special, that the fairies had wanted me for their own. This was a mistake, showing my innocence, my weakness. I was too old to believe in fairies, they said. Too old not to know that mothers lie.

"But she wasn't you," she goes on, when I don't respond. "I looked into those big baby eyes and I saw absolutely nothing."

I focus on crunching the lettuce between my teeth, the sting of vinegar on my tongue. I wish for a piece of bread, crusty on the outside, soft and white in the middle, to soak up what's left of the dressing. But bread is forbidden in our house now. It's for my own good, my mother tells me, cupping my cheek in her hand. I know she's measuring the fat there, feeling for the bone underneath.

"She didn't cry," my mother says softly.

I cry all the time. I cried this afternoon, when Angus Dormand stole my notebook and read it out loud to the kids on the bus. All those humiliating fantasies, strewn between the seats like spilled Cheetos and crushed into neon grime. Love poems punctuated here and there with an awful, damning she.

"They come from the woods," my mother says. "So that's where I went to get you back."

Last year, I tried to tell her. I stood in the doorway of her bedroom and said, "I think I'm gay."

My mother looked up at me, her eyes bright and tender, and said, "Oh, sweetheart," and for a moment I thought she would say she loved me no matter what. "Is this because you think you're not pretty enough to get a boyfriend?"

She pulled me into a hug. I couldn't move.

"Don't worry, baby," she said. "This diet is going to work wonders, you'll see. And once you're down a dress size or two, we'll get your hair done and buy some nice new clothes. All the boys will want to take you out."

That was three diets ago. So far, no wonders have been worked, but my mother never gives up hope.

"I carried that baby out into the woods. It was so cold, but she didn't cry, she just kept staring at me with those empty eyes. I set her on the ground, and she still didn't make the slightest noise. And I built a fire."

I think about the poem I ripped from my notebook, the one Angus read out loud. *Her fingers like mist, her mouth on mine a thundercloud.* After I tore it out, I shoved it in my mouth and let the paper turn to mush on my tongue. This salad tastes like that. I chew until I can't taste anything, then swallow the nothing. My stomach clenches, like an empty fist.

"I knew the fairy mother wouldn't let any harm come to her baby," my mother says. "So I picked it up and held it over the fire." She shakes her head. "I almost stopped right there, because what if I was wrong? What if I was about to hurt my real baby? But I looked that creature in its eyes and I knew it wasn't you. And I let go."

I can imagine the heat of the flames with perfect clarity, the smell of woodsmoke rising into the cold damp air. My mother's look of stony determination. There's some truth to this story, after all. She'll do anything to get her real daughter back, her right daughter, the daughter she should have had. She'll burn away all the parts of me that aren't supposed to be.

"The baby fell," my mother says, and even though she's told this story a thousand times her voice goes quiet and reverent. "And then it stopped falling. For a second, I thought it was hovering in the air, until I saw the hands that caught it. I couldn't make them out at first, because they were the same color as the forest at night."

This part of the story was my favorite as a child. My mother turning her head slowly to find a shape beside her, like a woman, but stranger, softer, melting at the edges. Her skin was blue or black or green, her mouth like an enormous knothole in a tree, and within—

"There you were," my mother whispers.

I know none of this happened, but I still wish I could remember it. My mother taking me carefully from the fairy's mouth, trying not to let her fingers brush the gnawing bark. My mother kissing my soft cheeks, frosted with tears. Carrying me home in the warmth of her arms. Lying awake all night to watch my face, to make sure I was never lost to her again.

Dessert is avocado pudding. Flavored with chocolate and cinnamon, it still tastes like nothing but green sliming the back of my throat. I'm so hungry, but I can't swallow another bite. "May I be excused?" I ask. She beams at me for leaving food on the table.

In my room, I light a candle that claims to smell like pumpkin pie, something I've never tasted. The scent that fills the room is warm and spicy-sweet, and I think about scraping the softening wax with a fingernail, placing it in my mouth.

Instead, I hold my hand high over the flame, then bring it down slowly, like lowering a flag. The heat is golden and lovely in the center of my palm until it sharpens and stings. I lower my hand further. The pumpkin-pie smell goes wrong, sugar burning at the edges. My arm trembles and in a second I'll have to flinch or scream—

Cool fingers lace through mine. The pain eases. I'm holding hands with a cloud.

She's here, under the trees where my bedroom wall used to stand. She's made of water and moonlight, with my round cheeks and hazel eyes. This isn't the mother, it's the daughter, the one who was supposed to be me. I recognize her from my love poem. Shadows roll down her face like teardrops.

Our fingers are still entwined. I don't know if she's here to steal me or save me, but I follow her without question. She leads me into the dark between the trees, where mushrooms grow in magic rings. I know you're never supposed to eat anything offered by a fairy, so I don't wait for her to offer. I kneel and pluck and bite. The flesh is warm on my tongue. A single taste fills me like nothing I've ever eaten.

Breaking another mushroom from its stem, I look up at her, my changeling, my shadow self. I hold out the mushroom, but she doesn't take it. She takes me, instead. She kisses me, and my heart grows a forest.

THE CAULDRON

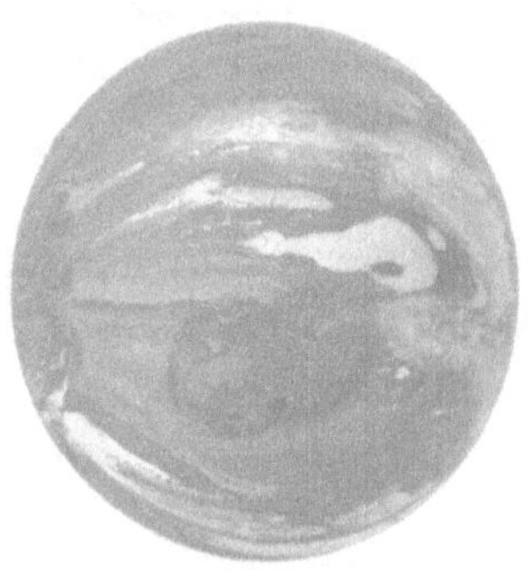

SIMO SRINIVAS

My esteemed colleagues warned me she would turn on me one day. *Erenay*, they said, *this is a fairy story. It cannot last.*

"Why?" I challenged them. "Because I am a witch?"

Yes, they said, *but more to the point, because you belong to the empire, and because you are a Turk and a Zanj. Your father was a Zanj and his father before him. This peace is fragile, Erenay, so be careful. Be watchful. She will turn.*

I didn't listen. We were in love. The witch and her princess. The witch and her queen.

And our son. We brewed him together.

†

We made certain that he would be known on sight, from the metallic thread of his hair and the jewels of his eyes and his teeth like two rows of pearls. No prince of woman born, sprung instead from a cauldron and a witch's spell.

He was made of all that was rare and beautiful that could be bought or stolen or compelled: pearls, rubies, sapphires, silks; a great gushing goblet of blood ennobled by centuries of careful inbreeding; and above all the infinite desire of his maker, his mother, our queen.

The cauldron was mine. A gift from the smith of my village in Anatolia. New brides took these squat iron vessels into the houses of their husbands, but with my father's blessing I carried mine to Vienna. In my academy years, I filled it with bread and coffee and flowers. During my exams, I made it bubble with acid, and with what proud delight did I convey it to my first posting in Bledawater!

When the princess of Bledawater came to see me in my cozy flat—the witch the empire had bestowed upon her, forced upon her—I let my cauldron steam with a little soup.

"Is it poison, Witch Irena?" she asked me. "Or a love potion?"

She smiled as she renamed me. I will never forget the soft black gleam of her eyes.

"It's supper," I said. And so: she joined me. And so: we fell in love.

†

OUR SON GREW in my cauldron. His mother grew stern. There was war in Bohemia, in Carinthia; there were spies in our midst. Anarchists bombed Bledawater Parliament and the Hexentreffen in Porosz. Separatists sent a golem to wring the Prime Minister's neck. My lover was afraid of the golems and persecuted their makers. *Erenay,* my colleagues said—witches all, in posts across the empire, sending their tidings by bird and wolf—*it has begun, she is turning.*

"Why shouldn't I turn?" my lover demanded. "I am a

descendant of Matthias Corvinus. I hear the voices of my people clamoring to be set free."

"But you suppress them," I said. "You condemn them and lock them in their homes. You draw false lines. These are my people, these are not. You define your borders with an iron wall and your country is now a cage."

"If you don't like it," she snapped, "you can go back to Zanzibar."

"Zanzibar?" I said, stung. "Because my father was a Zanj? No. My homeland is the steppe. The massif and the high plains and the salt of Tuz, the lake of glass."

My lover scoffed.

Erenay, my colleagues whispered, *your time is running out.*

After that, they no longer spoke to me. The tentacles of empire withered and withdrew.

†

HERE IS WHAT my lover's chosen people began to say of me: "Her father was the devil himself, a blood-drenched Moor. Her skin is as dark as her purpose, her hair is the night sky when hope and stars are lost; her eyes are burning pitch. She is the lying, spying, fork-tongued servant of outside forces, of evil forces that seek to destroy us."

Our nine months were at an end. As I lifted our son from the cauldron, my lover's soldiers came to kill me. She followed, dressed in the style of Matthew the Crow with a laurel wreath set upon flame-red ringlets. She looked at me through a sea of silver pikes with eyes as hard as coal.

"Unhand him, witch," she said.

Though it broke my heart, I did. She clutched him. She kissed him as if she were starving. She held him to her breast.

"*My* son! *My* heir!"

"For the rest of his life," I warned her, "he will be a

symbol of the obscene excess of the old regime. Each of his exquisite body parts could fund a nation. He will be hunted. You must take care."

"*You* will be hunted," my lover spat. "You, the Black Witch of Bledawater!"

My cauldron belched flame. We were gone from her in an instant, witch and cauldron, arriving smokily in the slums. For weeks, the golem-makers sheltered me while her soldiers combed the city. Then, combining our powers, we escaped together.

In Bukovina, we stole aboard a freight train to the East. After snow choked the rails, we walked and stumbled and crawled. We forded the Black Dragon River and circled west toward the steppe.

†

WHEN THE SUN rose over the plain in midsummer, I lifted my daughter from the cauldron. Half fair, half dark, mottled and misshapen: my patchwork princess, made of all the scraps her mother trimmed from her brother.

She has her mother's eyes. Her mother's name. One day, I will give her my cauldron.

Little news reaches us from the dictatorship of Bledawater. The steppe sings its own songs. Our horses tell their own stories. Fairy stories, they do not linger. They are carried away by the wind.

In the cauldron, there is grief. In the cauldron, there is the memory of fire.

Advice for Aspiring Cartographers

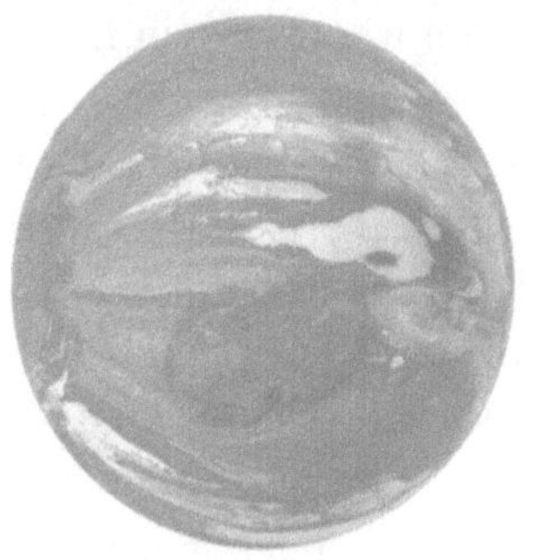

Avra Margariti

i.

Before you begin, you should know it's rotten work. Ask your fingers if they can bear to touch all the filthy kingdoms of the world. Ask them if they ever hope to wash off the stains.

ii.

There once was an unmoored, unmanned ship buccaneers sought through rope-coils of brume. Inside the phantom vessel, a driftwood altar—atop it a single tin mug. Dipping the mug into the sea to drink from the deep, teeth coated in saltwater communion, the pirates bit down on their tarnished blades and burst forth into battle believing themselves the once-and-future victors.

(The seabed had already built their graves.)

iii.

YOU MIGHT BE tempted to fog the edges of lands, make them
fuzzysoft, file away at their sharpness until your eraser is but a
stub and the monsoon-whorls of your fingers charcoal-dark.
  Don't.
  I can tell you right now that I chose to focus on the
sea and everything thereof. Let the eroded coastline be.
The serrated cliffs, slumbering underwater volcanoes, the
hollowed-out caves, too. The parts where people dug away
at the earth until their homes became islands, became
impenetrable forts.
  Learn to preserve the sharpness. Cut your fingers
against it all.

iv.

THERE ONCE WAS a man diving for sea sponges, sole
currency of his barren island. His boat mates watched
him leap overboard, counting the minutes his naked form
stayed under, a burly-chested chorus chanting hymns
passed down from old.
  A nomadic siren heard them, intrigued by the reversal
of roles. She drifted along the current of their melody and
found the diver fumbling on the seafloor, fingers scouring
seaweed and sand. With sun-streaked hair and earthen
skin, the man would look perfect in her anchor-chain of
tempted argonauts and fishermen.
  The siren keened her ethereal ballad louder than his
boat mates or his sponge-hungry hands, winding medusa
tendrils of hair around him. The diver slipped through
them as easily as a smelt escaping a badly-patched net.
He broke panting through the surface, arms full of porous
yellow sponges, their waterlogged bodies absorbing the
crashing waves of his heartbeat.

That night, he went home to his husband. Together they huddled by the fire, pressing curious fingers to mauvish sucker marks.

(The siren still waits, hoarse-voiced and empty-handed.)

v.

A CARTOGRAPHER IS a history-teller. There's something to be said for impartiality. You mustn't stretch or shrink borders, erase the blood soaked into the soil or flushed through the water like sharkbait. You mustn't be swayed by bright-eyed princesses ruling kingdoms by the ocean or foul-mouthed seafarers burning brighter than the imported cigars hanging off their fishhook lips. Sea serpents' tearful laments or savage shanties should not keep you up at night, should not make your ribcage feel as if it might crack open under pressure, mussel-like.

But when they do, keep vigil until morning, chasing the night with heady ale and stale hardtack.

vi.

THERE ONCE WAS a godling whose dominions were sand dollars, sun dogs, and other precious, fleeting things. They fell in love with a sailor's wife, goddess of climbing up steep rocks, staring at storm-tossed waves, and waiting for white homecoming sails (but always fearing the funerary-black ones).

The godling considered tickling Boreas' nose with a seagull feather until he sneezed, blowing the husband's homebound ship off course. They thought about the woman joining their coral-crimsoned domain, to create sea glass out of broken beer bottles and nacreous pearls out of sand grits by their side for all their windswept eternity.

I want you, the words lodged like a fish bone in their throat. The godling watched from their cumulus cloud. They saw their own longing reflected in the woman's eyes turned seaward. Goddess of waiting, of bow-legged body buffeted by the elements, of lighting candles every night to half-forgotten patron saints of please, please don't drown.

And so the godling took to the sea with their nebular boat, directing echolocation prayers to dolphins: please save this dreadful mortal, this would-be drowning man, please let him mount your grayslick backs.

They didn't stay for the happy couple's reunion.

(The godling had no desire to fathom the fleetingness, the permanence, the salinity of their own heartbreak.)

vii.

LET'S TALK ABOUT scale, about the mountains and pebbles, the sperm whales and amoebae. It's easy to lose yourself, be rendered a shipwreck with no tincture or ornate-labeled phial to chug down and become you again. It's easier still to see the blade of seagrass or lucky-charm black coral and miss the reef.

The flying fish cackle to one another, a maritime limerick about your hubris, moving your creations across an enamel chessboard. 1:1 million. Smaller, bigger, no?

Pick your ratio carefully.

Who will you exclude from your history of this watery world?

viii.

THERE ONCE WAS a selkie who stole her own skin before any suitor could snatch it She buried her seal-hide with its memory far away so that she couldn't find her old self if she tried.

The fish nibbled on her shrugged-off pelt, the birds' beaks plucked the fish, and up the food chain she went until a speck of her could be found in every crevice of the world.

The selkie roamed freely the shores and pelagi. She mingled with man and creature, woman and beast. In old age, in an island hospice, with oil-spill cancer on her too-human skin, the selkie remembered her former seal-hide: her insulation from the world, the aegis shielding the marvels of uncharted territories from view.

She thanked the fish, squid, and albatross. Before she slept at last, the primordial lullabies of seals singing her down, she spared a thought to her old lovers as well.

(I may have been one of them.)

ix.

Before you buy all the requisite instruments—your compass, sextant, and vernier, your parchment, ink, and pinion quills, your books of astral navigation—make sure you have what it takes stored up inside your hold. There are things that cannot be unetched from one's veins and ventricles.

Let me tell you about the blueprint inkstains, the callouses and cramps, the salt-encrusted eyes, the rocking boats and whale-fat oil lamps. Perhaps the mainland would be kinder on you. Pick up your graphite nib and sketch a forest that has never felt the sea breeze on its oaken skin.

The ocean is known for its mercurial undertows. You must have a sturdy pair of lungs to bask in the waves' rippling light.

x.

At night, I listen to the sea and all the tales the lapping waves whisper to me. Sometimes, I wake up, the wind an open-palmed slap against wet cheeks. There's something to be said for staying. You learn to love the accumulated barnacles, the ink that never seems to wash out.

And in return, when the time comes, place your trust in the water to lick you smooth and clean.

COLD TOUCH

DEVON BORKOWSKI

THE GIRL WAS splayed on the grass between two Honey Locusts, their yellow leaves like sunspots on bluing skin. She sat up at the clunk of the dorm door falling shut. Her head bobbled side to side, a sort of full body waving. He waved back. He didn't want to seem rude.

The girl had been there on and off all semester. She had been a nuisance earlier on, when she was still wailing past quiet hours, and grabbing at anyone who got too close. The RA had to call campus security twice. They came with night sticks and pouches full of salt; none of the students were supposed to leave their rooms until it was over.

She was quieter, after the second time, but she didn't really go away.

"I forgot my key, can you let me in?" she asked.

He pushed the toe of his sneaker into the dirt. "Pro'lly not, no."

"Why?"

"Don't think the RA would be super cool with it."

Most of the Ivies had ghosts, any campus that had been around long enough. Faded old codgers from so long ago you couldn't make out their faces. Just a shape, defined by high collars or the watery impression of a starched ruff.

This one wore corduroy shorts and a crop top. There were clovers poking out along her hairline, and one on her cheek where a pimple used to be.

"I forgot my key, I think I left it in my room. I'm trying to get back to my room."

"I know. I'm really sorry." And he was. Just not sorry enough to risk her hurting someone.

"Room two thirty—"

"I wish I could help. Honestly, I really do."

He didn't want to know her old room number. Didn't want to know any more than could be avoided. They all got an email from Res Life, after the second visit from campus security. *For the safety of all students, please avoid engaging the apparition whenever possible.* It made her stronger, they said. She'd start to fade the more people forgot her, and become less active in time.

He knew a few of the bleeding heart freshmen had taken offense on her behalf. They'd looked into deaths in the dorm and found her—her name, and how she died. They talked to her every time they passed, wrote her name in chalk across the front stoop. Maybe they were right, maybe she deserved that. But deserved didn't have a lot to do with it, in his opinion. He thought about the summer he turned thirteen, when he stood in front of the full-length mirror in his aunt's shore house guest room. He remembered the way that white tank top clung. Cupping the skin beneath it. Almost like something it was not.

Some things were best let go.

"It's a nice day out." Her head tipped to the side, loling at first, then meeting her shoulder with a *crack*. "Will you sit with me? For a little while?"

It was this or Expository Writing. He sat beside her on the ground, wet dirt clotting under his fingers. This close he could see the weeds poking through the tops of her thighs. She didn't smell like rot, not in the way he thought she might. More like ozone and cigarettes.

"You're pretty," she said.

He laughed. It wasn't something he heard often. He liked the sound, though. He felt the tickle of hair, the shaggy nape of his neck. *Pretty.* A word that smelled like sea breeze. He wiped his mouth, fingers catching on the rough snarl of stubble, and willed a half-formed longing away.

"Thanks. You were too."

She leaned in to put one cold hand over his. She kissed him, and it tasted like dirt, like bitter pine bark and leaf litter. Their teeth clicked, and hers gave—moving slightly in their loose sockets.

He pulled away."I gotta go, I'm late for class."

She didn't answer. She was looking at the dorm again.

"I forgot my key, could you let me in?"

Forte/Foible or

At the Center of Percussion

ASH HOWELL

YOUR BODY IS wrong; you were not made for violence.

Your eyes miss the edge-shine of the blade in the night. Your ears peal at the thunder of metal meeting metal; your tongue does not yet thirst for blood or know the taste of flesh.

These flaws could be forgiven, if not for your lies. Deceitful creature! You said your stomach was steel and your heart grown hard.

You dissembler—you try to hide the truth of yourself

MY BODY IS wrong; I was made for violence.

I am blind behind my back, but I know the knife is coming. My tongue hasn't torn and tasted like yours but why would it when my flesh is the feast, mangled in their mouths.

Survival requires adaptation: skin thickened, tongue quickened, guarding every part of a hardened heart—you'll get the truth I give you.

This artifice is honesty; the armor is more me than what you'd see beneath.

under artifice and armor and abdominals but I know you are as soft and red inside as everyone you and I cut open.

Your chest is a central sponge, frail lungs and friable ribs buried behind breasts. Your belly is indulgent, made for eating and laughing and making mewling things.

You are so afraid of dying.

I should have known then, I should have known when you lay bleeding and battered on the battlefield dying, dyed red, softness spilling out the same as all the rest.

You asked me how to live, as if I'd ever done it.

I said I did not know, and you said no you stupid fucking sword how do I live right now. You had held me so long, fought with me, thrust with me, trusted me as an extension of yourself.

I was made to rend, to end what I sink myself in. I was made to be hard and cold and unforgiving. This is honest: I was made for violence.

When I said let me in, you did.

The edge of you feels more real than guts opened up exposing soft red lies hiding inside. I am not like them.

My chest is a central sin, organs indifferent to appetite, the whole torso a transgression. The body betrays in myriad ways; you are not the only one regularly soaked in blood.

I am not afraid of dying; I am afraid of letting them win.

I could have died then, I could have died where they put me, dyed as red as you but less real. If I am disembodied, injustice must seek other souls to torment.

I've spent so long subsisting, I wonder what it's like to live.

You say you don't know, the only lie between us. You stupid fucking sword! I found you in a grave, silent, gave you violence, soaked you in soft red things, woke you to yourself.

You couldn't understand. Your form is your function; you are cold and hard and unforgiving. This is honest: a blade is made for violence.

When you said let me in, I did.

Now you will not be the soft thing you were. You will be cold and unforgiving. When I rended you I mended you, and we are soft and red but we will live. We will cut away our wrongness until we are made right.

Our body is violence, our body is wrong, our body is honest.

Now you are not so cold and unforgiving. You are soft; we don't like it. You examine the anatomy, see every evil angle. Your self ripped from our ribs will make us right.

Our body is violence, our body is wrong, our body is honest.

STEINWAY & HIS SONS

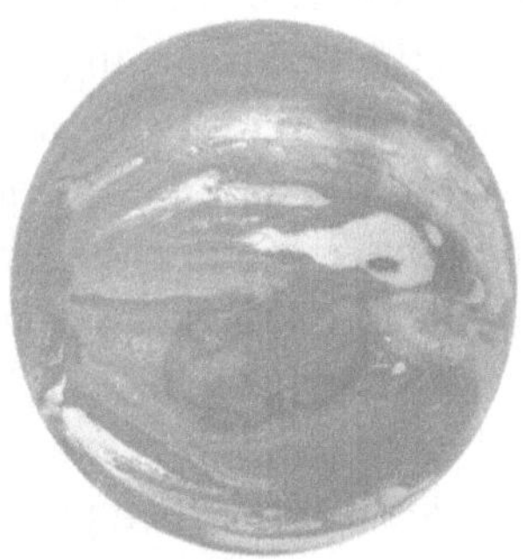

D.K. LAWHORN

HERE ARE ONLY two things your husband doesn't let go to ruin in the wake of you. One is the 6x8 framed picture of you both in Prospect Park on your third date. In the photo you squeeze each other close and smile into a phone camera held by a stranger who probably never spared another thought to either of you, let alone suspected their photography skills would be immortalized on your living room wall for forty-eight years.

This photo hangs to the right of the only other thing your husband is meticulous in his upkeep of: a Steinway & Sons Model S baby grand made of tiger mahogany. It has never budged from the corner he painstakingly directed the movers to place it, thirty-two years ago when it came home in the back of a Mercedes delivery truck without him informing you beforehand. Fresh off the showroom floor across the Hudson. You helped him clear out a space for it without question; he'd talked about how much he wanted a Steinway ever since you met him. Now he had one. The way he smiled when he uncovered the keys later that night was more than worth getting over your resistance to change, especially in things as fundamental as a living room layout. You fell asleep to beautiful renditions of Tchaikovsky and Bach, sitting to his right on the bench with your head resting on his shoulder. You awoke the next morning in your bed, tucked in snugly. When you walked to the living room in nothing but your Calvin briefs, you found him asleep at the piano, sitting straight up with his pretty chin resting against his chest, careful not to lean on the keys. You sat next to him on the bench and watched until his eyes fluttered open, your presence enough to tempt him out of the deepest sleep. He leaned in, kissed you, then played Brahms as you made coffee.

Now, when you sit on your side of the piano bench and watch your home turn into the hovel of a widower, it doesn't surprise you that the Steinway's corner seems repellant to mess. It does, however, shock you that there's trash piling up to begin with. Your husband was always the home keeper in the marriage. You were a bridge and tunnel businessman, working the ridiculous hours needed for a Black man to climb the corporate ladder in the Financial District. He was the premier Monacan concert pianist of the East Coast who only took a handful of gigs a year, though that handful always came close to equaling your yearly salary, bonuses included. He didn't mind being your little maid, though. He was a clean freak and liked the foreplay it often led to whenever you'd come home with a loose tie and undone top button to find him naked, dusting your study.

But even the shock of his fall into slovenliness doesn't compare to the day he sits down and begins to pluck out a melody on the Steinway you don't recognize. The new sequence of notes catches your attention and doesn't let go. You sit unmoving on the bench, in the indents left behind from all the years you spent beside him.

And you watch.

Your husband's long, bony fingers are unsure as they move across the keys. Every other note he hits is wrong in some mysterious but intrinsic way you cannot deny. But this doesn't stop him from going back and finding the correct one. He never writes down the music. He sleeps there on the bench, curled up with his head unknowingly in your lap, before starting from the beginning and playing every note perfectly all the way to where he left off the night before.

One morning, bathed in dusty rays slanting through the streaked Palladian window he installed himself as a ten-year anniversary gift, your husband begins by striking a perfect new note and stops. He cocks his head to the side, listening to it echo off the walls and junk surrounding him. Then he goes back to the start.

Your living room fills with runs, each gathering manic speed as hard-struck chords are followed by heart murmurs of caesuras that turn them lackadaisical. Crescendos build to a soul bursting head, until they reach a universal precipice, then a gentle decrescendo floats you back to earth like a leaf on the wind. Arpeggios follow with the dizzying step-like quality of Escher. All of this, strung together in your husband's precise order and immaculate precision, would've brought an entire music hall to a stunned silence. Finally, he plays the note he started the morning with. The sustain pedal draws it out; an indulgent fermata hangs in the air.

When the sound eventually disappears, your husband doesn't move.

You wait, watching those delicate, brown hands you know better than you knew your own. They hover above the keys, trembling. A sob rips out from his throat. Tears stream down his cheeks in crooked rivulets. Only then do you realize that you're crying, too—something you never thought possible. Not in your current state.

He wrote an original piece only once before and nearly dropped out of his undergraduate music program when his peers berated him for it being 'cliche' and 'trite' and 'just not that good'. He swore he would leave composition to the masters.

Fifty years later, the brain cancer hit you hard, and the hospital became your permanent residence. Fog fell over everything. Long periods passed where it was like you weren't even there. But he was there. Always. In a rare moment of clarity, you asked him to write a song on the Steinway. He promised to start on it that night and would play it for you once you kicked cancer's ass and came back home; a promise made as much for himself as it was for you.

You told him you couldn't wait to hear it.

But he didn't get the chance to go home that night. And then, with the funeral to plan, he kept himself busy and out of the house as much as possible. When he finally did sit behind the keys again, he found his finger numb and uninspired.

He stares at you now, meets your eyes. The corners of his lips pull back into a weak smile, making waves across the mahogany skin of his cheeks and folding his forehead along the four lines that have always been there but somehow never wrinkled. It's been years since you've seen that smile.

I'm sorry it took so long to keep my promise.

You see, I felt you come home with me the day I left your body at the hospital. But it took a while to be sure I hadn't gone crazy. Your imprint never leaving the bench cushion gave all the confirmation I needed. I won't tell anyone. And I won't play this song I crafted for anyone else. I'm fine with that.

After all, I wrote it just for you and me and Steinway and his sons.

MONOLOGUE

KENGO NELSON

$\mathcal{A}$s Aldebaran's outer layers were shed and gradually revealed the white dwarf beneath it, Will and Gale transformed Taurus Crossing into a thriving tourist destination. Wayward voyagers stayed at the station for weeks, sometimes months, to witness the shift: the slow reveal of the pale light beyond the gasses scattering across the solar winds. The station's brilliant mirror panels became a beacon for travelers, leading their eyes to the station's trademark sign: *See The Star, See The Show.*

"Tonight's show will be wonderful, Will. I'm sure of it."

Gale crossed the lobby from the entry port, his metallic feet thumping less than gracefully against the threadbare carpet covering the dust-heavy floor. Slowly, steadily, the android made his way up the staircase, still the centerpiece of the station theater's spacious lobby, and through the red and gold double doors leading to the mezzanine.

At its greatest peak, Taurus Crossing welcomed millions of travelers from across the universe, all for the spectacle of the station's revue and the once-in-a-lifetime chance to watch a star's decay. Taurus Crossing was Will's passion project, and Gale had delighted in keeping it running with him. Will brought artistic vision to the revue: selecting starlets, conceptualizing costumes and choreography, and training talented comics and dancers who went on to become stars in their own right. Gale handled logistics: finances, scheduling, announcements, and everything else needed for Will's ideas to flourish.

But when only the white dwarf remained, visitors and performers alike abandoned the station, searching for the next great spectacle of the universe.

Gale had felt a *shift* when moving his mechanical limbs that morning, one that had been coming for centuries, so he put himself to work. He manually pulled up the stage curtain—its lifting machinery stopped working long ago—then opened the doors to the station's deteriorating theater foyer to beckon non-existent travelers in to see the star, to see the show.

Once done, Gale trudged along the arcing hallway behind the mezzanine until he reached a private box just off stage right, where two seats had been reserved for millennia. It took more effort than he ever remembered expending to shift his stiffening joints, metal interior scraping against itself to finish the trip. As he settled into his familiar seat, the weight of lifetimes sank into his body, feeling more like relief than anything else.

Behind the stage, the station's brilliant two-way mirror panels provided the same spectacular view of Aldebaran it always had, the star's pale light glimmering across the stage and into the orchestra seats.

Will had been silent since the station finished its 500th lap around the white dwarf. By then, the show had not had an audience for hundreds of years. Gale slowly extended his left arm out to place his hand on top of Will's long-silent android shell, resting right where he had wanted to be in his last moments.

"I can't wait to see the show with you again."

Right where they'd agreed to spend forever together.

When Gale's core started to flicker, he cleared his throat one final time.

"Esteemed guests, travelers, friends…one and all… we welcome you to Taurus Crossing. The spectacle of Aldebaran…awaits you, so please take your seats… mind…your fellow audience…members and…enjoy… the…"

HOW I DID NOT MAKE FRIENDS WITH TENIEL EU LETXIE

BREE WERNICKE

TWO DRINKS, AND I start telling people I can do syokk. Is that entirely accurate? No. Can I stop myself? Also no.

The party is at my frenemy Eurli's flat, and she air-kisses me hello as I push a bottle of my least favorite brandy at her. "Didn't you bring anyone?" she asks, but fuck if I'm going to knowingly inflict Eurli on another human being. I shrug at her and escape to the drinks rack. I don't recognize anyone here so this'll suck unless I start talking to people, and fast. I hi-my-name's-Gebrenie-what's-yours around the place until I wind up in a circle of people sprawled on cushions, one-upping each other.

Well *I* had my very first paper published in *Magic*.

Well *I* got that grant for thaumoquantum transference, trials begin in City Brenetxie next month.

Well *I* just got off the waitlist for a Triu Tetxe wand.

"Oh, you're all magicians," I say.

Nods all around. "Aren't you, Gerit?" someone says.

"Gebrenie," I say. "No, I never picked it up properly. But I did learn a little something when I was younger." Not the Brenetxie magic they're talking about, though.

"Aw, show us then!"

"Yes, you must!"

Credentialed magicians love nothing so much as watching an amateur struggle.

"Couldn't possibly," I say, because you have to, but I set my drink on the floor, because I am a showoff.

"We can give you some tips," one of the magicians says sweetly.

"Loooove tips," I say. But instead of pulling a cheap wand out of my bodice, I close my eyes and lock my hands together. And—my mind blanks.

Oh shit oh fuck. Did I really forget how to start?

I haven't *really* done syokk in over a decade. I tell myself I can still do it if I want to, because it'd be sad if I couldn't. I used to love it. I still love it. But do I practice? Nah. It's depressing practicing alone and I can hardly show up to the Cultural Center Ingaraadie on my own, looking obviously Ebrenetx. What would I even say—"Hi, I swear I'm not a total weirdo with an unseemly interest in your traditions! I just learned syokk when I was young and want to practice!"—which sounds suspiciously like something a total weirdo would say.

Somewhere in the midst of my drunk blanked-out panic my second-year teacher's voice floats into my head. *Start with breath. Go as slow as you need to.* She's speaking Tuibrenetx, not Ingaraapk, which isn't right, but hey. It works. I remember, and I breathe. The sensation gathers between my palms. I open my eyes to a froth of cinnamon-colored light around my fingers, shapeless and faintly warm.

Fuck, I'm rusty. The light is supposed to be clear and strong, not…bubbly. But it's workable. I poke and prod at it until it starts reacting, like a glob of taffy. Draw out a glimmering, uncooperative neck, and a set of fins because triangles are easy, and then I have something like…a giraffe shark? Not fancy. Just a stupid party trick. Magic from a place that never wanted me anyway.

The magicians have gone silent and stony, the syokk-light glazing their faces dark red. One girl's leaning forward, something sharp in her eyes. With a jolt, I recognize her.

"You know syokk," she says.

Teniel eu Letxie. We've only met once before, but I know more about her than I should. We run in the same circles. Not friends—yet. Online she's pretty loud about Ingaraadz politics. (She's half, Eurli told me last week. The famine brought her grandparents all the way here. And they're dead now.) Teniel probably does gorgeous syokk. Builds whole myths out of light one-handed. And here I am with a lumpy little glob. She's about to tear me apart.

"Only a little," I protest.

Her gray eyes bore into me. "How'd you learn?"

Online class, an Ebrenetx might say. Saw a traveling exhibition and became enamored of the art. Ingaraadie stuff is just so cool, you know?

"I, uh, I learned it in primary school. In Ingaraad," I explain. A more legitimate reason than most Ebrenetx have. "I grew up there. Well, almost. Not entirely. Just a few years." (Two. Barely.) "Then we moved back here." Teniel's not saying anything. My syokk begins to flicker. "But, uh, yeah, in school we did syokk every morning, after math. I'm not very good anymore, as you can see, but uh…" I gesture vaguely with both hands, and my giraffeshark bobs along like a deflating balloon. "It's fun!"

Fun. I hate myself.

The magicians are getting up, making noises about drinks, but Teniel crawls onto my cushion. Oh no, she's going to clap in. I'll have to pull out all the stock patterns I still remember, and hope she gets bored before I drown in the light like the fraud I am. I grit my teeth and yank some Ingaraapk out of a dark corner. "Syokk-n lluwty?"

Shit damn fuck, wrong tense. *We practiced syokk?* I sound like a dumbass. Worse—she hasn't even told me she's Ingaraadz yet.

She just stares at me, and my will to live shrivels. I hope I black out and forget all of this.

"Sorry," I mumble. My giraffeshark falters and melts into nothing.

Teniel watches it go without expression and then says abruptly, "I can't even speak it. Let alone practice syokk."

Horrible relief. I almost laugh, but that'd be ghoulish. "Oh," I say instead.

"I didn't want to learn, growing up," she says. "And no one pushed me to. But now I regret it."

"You could still try," I say. "Online class?"

But we both know that's bull. Childhood acquisition windows and all that. You'd never get more than a tiny glimmer up, starting after age twelve.

"Or I can teach you what I know," I say, too eagerly. I shouldn't even care. Why do I care? It's weird that I care. "But, you know, like—I'm really bad now. I used to know way more. And it all—faded. And I don't know if I can ever get it back."

Teniel looks at me for several seconds too long. "Well, I never even had it at all," she says. "Your plesiosaur was cute, though." She drains her drink and rises from the cushion without a backward glance. "Good talk, Gebrenie."

In Brenetx, that's a friendly enough goodbye. In Ingaraad, it's *fuck you.*

I know which way she meant it.

Sailing the Ship of Theseus Across the Border

Leon Tomova

Thirteen minutes into my interview, the man in the murky green shirt asks me where I learned to speak English so well.

I deliver a sea glass smooth response and take a sip of my latte macchiato to wash back the frustration that swells in my throat. He already asked me for my references and I had to fumble through an explanation of why I didn't have them with me. I'm starting to stand out, and not to my advantage.

In the next lull of conversation, I excuse myself and go to the restroom.

I lock myself in a graffitied toilet stall and twist the knob on my nacre watch back until the two hands make a right angle between 9 and 12.

Normally, I wouldn't go more than an hour back, but I really need today to go well. I should have rewound when the mail person missed my delivery, but I hoped the references wouldn't come up. I can already hear the disapproval in my mother's voice when I call to tell her how the interview went and the three-hour loop comes up. *You're pushing yourself too hard,* she'll say, in the vaguely tinny buzz of several thousand kilometers of distance. The same thing she said when I coasted through exam season on energy drinks and trail mix, and the same response will rattle against the backs of my teeth: *I can't do this otherwise.*

Or maybe I just won't mention it.

I click the knob back into its groove and feel the familiar lurch of my stomach as reality twists under my feet and unspools. For a moment, I panic that I'll phase in while someone else is in the cabin, but then spacetime dons the trappings of light and matter like a well-loved hoodie slept in one time too many and I'm standing in the same stall, blessedly alone.

I take a long breath. The smell of bleach burns the inside of the cheek that I've chewed raw in my anxiety.

I open the door. A middle-aged woman touching up her lipstick yelps at the person with the short hair and unisex slacks who emerges from a stall that was previously unoccupied. I give her a tight smile, which seems to dispel her alarm.

I step in front of the mirror when the woman's freed it and use some water to smooth my undercut back into shape. I've yet to find a gel strong enough to withstand time travel.

When I leave the restroom, the coffee shop is awash with rush hour activity. The table I took—will take in two hours and forty-five minutes—has been claimed by a blond man with wireless headphones and a tablet propped on his cappuccino cup.

I slink out without anyone noticing.

In the dappled sunlight outside, I pause to situate myself.

Stray mail easily tops my *Top 10 Reasons to Time Travel* list. Subleasing an apartment comes with an assortment of loopholes to wiggle through; having mail delivered to a mailbox that doesn't have your name on it is among the worst of them. Especially when you're waiting for time-sensitive paperwork.

My bike is not at the stand in front of the coffee shop—I haven't arrived, and will not arrive here for another couple of hours—so I power walk to the subway station. The train is so full that there's little I can do but cling to the handrail for dear life, but as soon as I'm back aboveground, I pull up the shipment details on my phone. I have fifteen minutes to get home before the delivery person.

I'm down to seven by the time I reach my apartment. I fish a notebook out of my bag and tear out an empty sheet. I write the tracking number and the correct mailbox in big blocky letters, then find some washi tape in the depths of my pencil bag and stick the note to the door. I don't go upstairs—my three-hours-younger self is still in the apartment, and I must not come too close to them. People like me are essentially metaphysical ships of Icarus: rebuilding and replacing ourselves with the parts that help us stay on course. And you can't have two ships sailing on the same current.

My note does the trick. The mail person comes; the envelope is deposited in the mailbox; a green checkmark in the tracker informs me that the delivery has been finalised.

Now I'll have my references.

There's one more thing I need to do here before I can go to my interview.

I tear a second sheet from my book and write a well-practiced note on it before I fold it into a little boat. I open the mailbox and take the thick envelope, leaving the boat in its place. I wonder how Theseus would feel about his ship if he was one of the parts that could be replaced. I head to the nearby coffee shop to kill time before my interview.

The truth is: there can be only one me. Technically, there is only one; I'm a rope wrapped around itself in a figure-of-eight, but at this crossing point, we are two. Which is why the me who's still back home will find a paper boat in their mailbox with *blagodarya ti* written on the inside. They'll take a long walk, grab something to drink. Then they'll kick back and wait for spacetime to right itself and swallow them in its tide.

I hope it's a good way to go.

I try not to think about what this all says about me: that the version of me that's closest to perfect is the one that's sent away all the wrong ones. Or what will happen when I find a paper boat among my own things.

When I enter the coffee shop, the cute barista is bringing out a tray of muffins—three blueberry, three chocolate. He greets me with a smile that ripples in my chest cavity. He's a foreigner too, evidenced in the smooth edges of his vowels and the way he lights up when I let some of my own accent spill. I order a medium drink and he makes me a large. I get one of the muffins. I debate giving him my number, decide against it, then think about a braver version of myself circling back from the future to replace me, and I scribble it on a cup sleeve. Perhaps he could make something of all the ship pieces that don't quite fit together.

I arrive for my interview with my references at the ready and the man in the murky green shirt stands up to greet me. "Welcome," he says. "I'm glad you could make it."

The Perils of Mimicry

ERIN ROCKPORT

I AM NOT LEAH Donovan.

I look just like her. I have her hair—dirty blonde, ramrod straight—and her green eyes. I am the right height and weight to fit her clothes exactly. I've got her freckles and even the little scar on her chin from when she fell playing tag in the fourth grade.

But I am not Leah Donovan.

I am the thing that took her place.

Leah had a family. She had parents, friends, a partner—but none of them noticed when I stepped into her life. One day she was there, and the next I had taken her place, and not one of the people who loved her remarked on a difference.

I fit her life like a glove. I go to her job, a menial secretarial role at a health clinic. I have dinner with her parents. I sleep next to her girlfriend. Leah had to deal with complications like *stress* and *attachment* and *feelings*. I have none of these to contend with. I can work endlessly, mirror any emotion, slip into any situation.

Her boss is overjoyed. Her friends are thrilled that I come to every outing, her parents remark how lovely it is to see me every weekend. I take her girlfriend out on dates every week, buy her gifts, fuck her sweetly. I inhabit Leah's life better than she, messy and human, ever could have.

And yet.

And yet.

Despite my perfection, despite my superiority, Leah's life begins to unravel around me.

It starts small. I order a burger when out with Leah's best friend, and she questions my choice; Leah had been a vegetarian. The next weekend, her mother retrieves a photo album of an old vacation. I don't feel anything about the pictures; I can't. Her mother doesn't hide her disappointment at my blank expression, and I excuse myself to the bathroom.

"Does Leah seem a little off?" she asks when I am out of the room, a half-whisper clearly not meant for me.

Her father rumbles agreement. "A bit strange, sure. She's been working a lot recently, maybe that's why."

When I return, they say they want to take a break from weekly dinners.

Leah's friends begin to withdraw. I attempt to speak about topics of mutual interest—work, recently-watched television shows, idle gossip—but only receive frowns and changes of the subject in response. They are unnerved by me. I sit while they talk amongst themselves, a broad smile plastered onto my face.

I am smarter, faster, funnier—I know every script and every rule and I am prepared for any outcome. I'm superior to Leah. So I strap the smile on harder, sink deeper into Leah's skin, and attempt to ignore the crawling wrongness as I push forward. I hold tightly to every sliver of connection.

Still, the invitations from her friends recede. I am an unwanted companion, an awkward silence. I don't understand it.

My performance at work suffers. I continue to push myself beyond a regular human's breaking point, but it does not bring her coworkers closer to me. Leah's clothes begin to feel stiff and itchy against me, and I cannot tell if it's because they are too small or because I am too big. The world becomes noisier.

It is her girlfriend's rejection that cuts most deeply, because I have been the *perfect* partner. Leah had a temper: she could be selfish, childish, overly emotional. I am undemanding, uncomplicated. I ask for nothing.

"You're different," she says when I come home to find her bags packed. "I don't understand why, but you are."

I say, "Don't go. We can work this out."

She shakes her head, tears falling freely. "I don't think you mean that. I don't even think you love me anymore."

"Of course I do." The words ring hollow even to my own ears.

"I don't think you love *anyone* anymore. You're empty."

After she leaves, the apartment is so terribly quiet. I pull at Leah's memories, sure that I must have missed something for her life to have worn thin so quickly. Surely I have done everything I can, fulfilled every role to the best of my ability?

In Leah's memories, her parents embraced her warmly, told her they were proud of her. Her friends laughed at her jokes, exchanged genuine pieces of themselves in stories. Her girlfriend touched her softly, eyes so full of tenderness that the recollection scorches me. I never received any of that.

Time passes, and the space around me becomes colder and emptier. The world becomes louder and harsher, more difficult to bear with nothing to shield me from the sharp, strident bleakness of it all. Soon there will be nothing left of Leah's life, and I will need to move on, to find another skin. Her friends and family will not miss me.

Because I am not Leah Donovan, and they will never love the thing that ate her.

A WINE GLASS OF MERCURY

ELENA SICHROVSKY

OPHELIA STIRS THE tiny wooden cauldron of salted peanuts with a finger before selecting one to nibble on. Lucifer tucks a strand of turquoise hair behind their ears and laughs with all their teeth, lips wet with cranberry juice. Even November, who's usually the quiet one, is gibbering away, both elbows on the counter. There's two empty Long Islands in front of her and the bartender is handing her a third.

Then my phone alarm goes off at a volume that's hard to ignore, a pinprick to the balloon of drunk, giggle-infested conversation.

"What's *thaaat*?" Lucifer sings, accompanied by a prodding finger.

"Nothing." I turn the phone over. "Just a reminder to take my lithium."

Ophelia frowns, her nickel-brown eyes widening. "The thing that's in batteries?"

"Of course Poms isn't going to eat batteries," November drawls, mouth half-open, as she attempts to touch her nose with the tip of her tongue.

"I-I'm not going to eat batteries." I fumble, rubbing a thumb across my jaw. "It's a-an antidepressant. Of sorts."

"My mom takes lithium, I think. She's bipolar." November presses her lips against the edge of the plastic straw. "Or Lamictal? One of the L-words."

"*Lovvvvve*," Lucifer croons, holding a peanut in their fist as an imaginary microphone.

The conversation balloon swells back to its spherical shape. My friends carry on, not noticing—just as they never have—how I start to shift from one butt cheek to the other, how I roll my shoulders back and forth as the bone sockets squeak.

I need to get home and take my lithium. Two hours past deadline is the maximum I can endure.

The night comes to an end after Lucifer vomits in the men's bathroom stall and we each take a turn to wet a napkin and blot the bits of regurgitated fries off their salmon blouse. Lucifer and November take one cab, and I share another with Ophelia, who's tipsy-crying in the hem of her sweater and mumbling about a dead bird she saw outside the gas station two weeks ago.

In the dark of the backseat of the car, while Ophelia presses snot stains into my shoulder, I reach down between my legs and detach my labia.

"Poms," Ophelia murmurs, her breasts dipping against mine. "I think the birdie might've been s-scared." She hiccups. "Birdie is scared."

I move my hand out of the shadows and pat the slant of her shoulder blade. "It's okay, Phe. It's okay."

When we arrive outside her apartment, I gently pry her off me until she finally exits the car with a delighted whoop and a wave.

As soon as my foot crosses into my bedroom, I rip my right shoulder blade out of its socket before I'm even fully undressed, then dig my thumbs into the hooks around my butt cheeks so I can toss them aside. The breasts land in the laundry basket, the scalp into the half-open closet door. The vagina I put carefully into the drawer beside my bed; it's custom-made. Expensive.

I flop out on the bed, now nothing but a torso with a left arm and a ragged neck. I exhale.

Silvery-blue wires start streaming out of each amputated orifice. They wiggle and worm across the cotton bed sheets, practically ecstatic. My remaining arm digs for the packet of batteries under my pillow and I pop a single black and orange striped AAA into the open socket at the top of my neck.

The wires hum in contentment, gripping and releasing the bed sheets tenderly.

My breathing flattens to a soft murmur, tight coils unfurling in sweet relief. A few more wires tumble out from the tunnels my legs used to be attached to. They reach across the mattress like a slow trickle of honey slipping down the fur of a black bear's chin.

I return the batteries back under my pillow. The allure of downing the entire pack always lingers in the back of my mind, but then so do the consequences. I remember the time my vagina clattered to the floor while a man's hands were in my hair. There was also the workplace incident (imagine my breasts squeaking when my boss' brother grabbed them), and that dismal Monday when my legs sprang loose and bounced down the stairs right before I gave a presentation on energy-saving mineral alternatives.

By now I've taught myself to resist the urge to splurge and take just one every night. So I can stand upright without fear of my appearance cracking; so I can get comfortably fucked in every custom-designed genitalia hole; so I can taste desire and disgust and watch sweat collect on brows like frog eggs.

And then I come home and dismember the fabrication. I love November, Lucifer, and Ophelia, but they only know me in the capacity I create for them to perceive. What would they think of me now, a chest split open and sleek wires spilling like spaghetti over obsidian black silk sheets? I am an airborne screensaver, I am a bouquet of earphone wires, I am a painting you think you created but then are disappointed to realize only ever existed in a dream.

I might be your disappointment, but I am my own divinity. I am what I am without the intervention of arbitrary criteria. I am a wine glass of mercury with a tin-foiled lipstick smear on the edge.

I sprawl out on my bed, thinking about electric pylons and the slenderness of their one thousand fingers reaching inside to touch me. With a shudder my final arm comes loose from its socket. It falls to the side as I picture myself grinding up and down the pylon's cusp, electricity thrumming through me. My wires trill and twinkle; they flood the mattress and dangle over the sides, glittering in the overhead light like comets slipping from the gaps between God's fingers.

The Six Most Common Questions Asked by Customers in Rubian Brothels

MORRIS HINKLE

1. *"Freshly molted?"*

IF IT'S NOT the first question, it's the second. They prefer us soft. I think they think we're helpless fresh out of a molt. I think that makes them feel more in control.

I always tell them yes. They don't know the difference. I know workers that pluck the hairs from their carapace and file down the sharp points of their spines. They don't know our bodies well enough to see the lie. We could be a week from our next molt and the customer would still believe us, so long as we pretend with them.

There are those of us that take a different route. Honored never files its points or plucks its hairs. It takes customers only late in the molt when it is at its hardest.

"They pay for dangerous," Honored tells me. "They like to be scared."

On a good day, I say I am not as brave as Honored. When the hunger grips my mandibles I say that I am not as willing to lie. It's not fair to say it. Honored lies, yes, but no more than I do. I say I do not hunger. It says I will not eat you, no matter how hungry I may be. Neither of us dare to get anywhere near the truth.

2. "Are you a girl?"

IF IT'S NOT the second question, it's the first. As if those words mean anything to me. As if categories created for another species could ever fit our forms.

I lie. Sometimes I say I am female because it's obvious what they want. Sometimes I say I am male just to see what they'll do. Sometimes I tell them that I am a surprise for them to unwrap.

They like it when I say this. I do not. There is something rotten about taking a truth and wrapping it in so much webbing that the shape of it is lost. It feels like the worst lie of them all.

3. What's your name?

I AM THE six hundred and seventeenth Graciousness. The teachers recognized me before I had even begun my first molt. Many have journeyed to see me after we were separated by death, loving me for the Graciousness I no longer remember being but once was. The six hundred and fifteenth Graciousness, I am told, was one of the first cosmonauts. The three hundred and twelfth Graciousness's deeds are why my likeness is hung in the Great Hall for all to venerate. It is a source of pride to know that I have been a part of this community for thousands of years, the continuation of an unbroken and meaningful lineage.

I tell them my name is Sweetness.

If there is one of us named Sweetness, I have not met it, but I have met many who use the name. I do not know how it started. Maybe one of us took the name in the early days and it became an expectation.

In its own way, being a Sweetness is a lineage as long and proud as being a Graciousness. This is what I tell myself when I hear the name drip from their mouths like secretions. This is what I pray I would have understood in my last life and will still believe in my next.

4. *"Will you marry me?"*

SOME OF US forget that they are dangerous.

"He's kind," Trembling told me. "He's generous, and thoughtful, and always asks after me."

There is a story that is repeated often and in many ways. It goes like this. One of us falls in love with one of them. He brings it home. It tries to fit in.

In one ending it starves to death, repressing the hunger so long that it no longer remembers how to eat. In another, it eats its so-called husband, unable to hold back as the hunger grows heavy on its mandibles. In most tellings, the family kills it before it can do either of these things.

We lie, all the time. Sometimes we forget what is real and what is not. Sometimes we forget that no matter what kind of connection we forge between our worlds, no matter how many of our points we file and hairs we pluck, to them we will never be anything but alien.

Honored tells the story often. In its version, the family finds it fresh from a molt and, starving, eats it.

What do we know about their habits? Perhaps, in their own way, they are as ravenous as us.

5. *"Why do you do this?"*

"IT'S TRASHY," FERVENT tells me often. "You're flattening

us out into their shape. You act like our being, our world, is something they can buy." If Fervent has ever lied, it wasn't in this life.

Truth is a molt splitting in two, a softer form squeezing from the crack. Truth is the pulsing stupor that grips me after I molt, the way days pass without me noticing at all. Truth is the frenzied hunger that comes when I awake.

Truth, if truth be told, is an untranslatable thing. They will never understand what I am. I will never understand what they want. I can only give them an approximation, and they can only comprehend the lie.

The teachers used to chide us for eating our molts. It isn't good for you, they'd say. There is nothing left but air and crunch.

At least I feel like I'm eating something. At least I can convince myself, in my insatiable hunger, that I will not starve.

6. *Have you ever eaten a human?*

YES. MANY TIMES, you stupid, soft man. I have eaten many humans and I would eat many more, except I do not want to be pulled into the street and dismembered like the six hundredth and twenty-seventh Raucous, or hunted down like the five hundredth and ninety-eighth Fervent. It is a thin and fragile thing that holds the hunger in my mouth and away from your flesh.

This is, of course, a lie.

I, too, prefer my partner to be freshly molted. I, too, feel more in control when I believe them to be helpless. I would not eat you, I say, and this lie is as much for them as it is for me. They listen to the *would not* and feel the triumph of special treatment. I listen to the *eat you* and let myself believe I am more dangerous to them than they are to me.

There is a story repeated often and in many ways. It goes like this. The customer shows a video, or an image, or explains in great detail about a creature on their world that looks something like us. He calls it a *spider*, or a *scorpion*, or a *creepy-crawlie*. He calls it small. He calls it frightening.

They don't scare me, he says. They're not that hard to kill. But you're different. I'm more scared of you than you are of me, aren't I?

And the worker opens its mandibles, leans towards the man, and lies.

WHO NEEDS IT?

LIZA WEMAKOR

I'VE LEARNED THAT I'm Yemaya's daughter, but it was hard for me to believe when my messenger told me. How could I be of her when I'd always found love so elusive, and I'd long called Spinster Street home?

I didn't understand that Spinster Street was full of love even though its residents were single. Yemaya, She works in mysterious ways. Even in my loneliness I was making love. It's no wonder that I thought about it all the time.

All I ever wanted was love, even when I thought I was without it. I needed the reach toward love, even when I seemed to fall short of it. Hell yes to stretching into clumsy flirtation or too-soon confessions so those of us who still feel new to this might have higher chances at easy mushy profusion, the sweet teasing drags that turn lovers on at night. There's a mad science to it. Nothing is possible before there's a reach and the first lives ever were, I think, side effects of particles shooting their shots. If you wanna know about romance, spend time where I lived, on Spinster Street, where people dance without partners because they've tapped the core of romance—they're often in love and ready for more if it comes.

In September 1998, when New York was getting chilly, I walked through a cloud of it. Fragrant laundry steam from a townhouse basement mistified the exit from Church Ave station and through the blur I spied the silhouette of a suave fellow wearing a jean jacket with the lapels turned up and a *smooth* ass Bronx accent that seemed to be dyed burgundy. I still smelled like the dive bar I tended—like a drinker and a chainsmoker. Like problems. And there was this calm fellow, blasting hardcore shit on their walkman. I heard the bass of Biggie Smalls' voice through their headphones. Then the fellow smiled at me and I was 42 and they were 39 and I smelled like problems, and we were getting older, and I wasn't the most lookworthy woman on the street even at that time of night, and I'd never been in love and I'd only had sex once, I was a black sheep with few prospects, and I wasn't their type and they weren't mine, but they turned their head and I liked the way they looked at me, and they liked my problems and how I couldn't walk as fast as them though my legs were longer and how I looked them dead in their face—in *this* city—though I knew better. And I liked the crow's feet on the otherwise moonlight smoothness of their face, and the silvers where their teeth had been knocked out in a fight, and their self-conscious chivalry and how nothing they said confused me, and the way they knew I was black and I knew they were white and it didn't hurt, and the way they pulled down their headphones and slowed their stride to talk to me, and the way they smoothed their thumb across my desert-dry palm before they wrote their number, and their name: *Van.*

Van and I had waited a long time for each other and I didn't believe they were here, didn't believe my lover was gonna be shorter than me with moonlight skin and a blonde bouffant. I made a point, when we met up for late-night springrolls after they got off from the warehouse in

December—I made a point, when they blew their warm air on my cold hands sending tremors down my body—I made a point of remarking on how perfectly content I was to never have lived for anyone but myself. *Love, who needs it?* I'd blurted out, and they said, *I do, I need it and I want it too,* and they looked up from under their thawing eyelashes, sending a gust through my chest, and as we walked to my place we were both very quiet.

It was easier for Van to sleep over at my place sometimes, less of a commute, trains could be scary that late at night, so they washed up in my bathroom and slept on the couch in their cute tank and boxers, and the light that came through cracks in the blinds would shimmer on their forehead just so, making it look like the moon, and I would kiss a bright spot on their dewy skin while they slept. I didn't make much of it, I made a point of not making much of it, I just had to do it, kiss their dewy forehead and whisper goodnight, sweet dreams and make the blanket snugger and adjust the pillow so it was supportive, but one night they caught me doing it and they touched their hand to the side of my neck, they blinked their thawed, corn silk eyelashes at me and bit their bottom lip and wanted me in my big t-shirt and my headscarf. And slowly they moved into my apartment and my life and I to their life, which they knew would happen all along.

One night they held me from behind and asked, "Diane, do you know what I am?"

I laughed. "The love of my life?"

They rubbed my back, cueing me to face them. "Do you know how we found each other?"

I laughed again and asked, "Good timing?"

The slow, desirous feeling in the room had changed—acquired a frenetic energy. Their smile flashed at me, silver teeth catching all of the light in an impish fashion.

Then they began glowing rose pink from hair to sole. It took several moments to process. Where they touched me,

I felt pink like them.

They murmured: "I have a reservoir of love inside of me. I am of Aenghus. Of Cupid. The gods of love, they sent us to each other. I'm fae."

I was fearful. Not because of what Van was, I've since understood, but because of what they recognized in me — expected of me. I never wanted to be distinctive.

Van showed no disappointment, only expectancy. *Think about it,* they asked. Once again I was made quiet.

Spinster Street. Was I responsible? Was it of my making? Did the lonely not only dance with me but because of me?

Van and I kissed tirelessly, and I licked their silver teeth, every inch of their mouth I could find. They tugged on my lips with their teeth until my skin felt like swollen fruit. An ocean blue shimmered above the brown.

This is what I'd been waiting for. I let Yemaya, Van and Aenghus use my body that night on the comfort of a second-hand mattress.

My head swam deliciously, in the sweet sea of realization.

I learned that I was fluid. Queer is good and bad and neither because, really, it is more of a quality figured by place and person and time, and that was what I had been all along: someone who fell outside the lines of my place and person and time, godly, transtemporal, neither here nor there.

I released my godly hold on Spinster Street that night, freeing residents to remain alone or find each other. Love was ours and it always had been, in single and coupled forms.

Moon Bearer

CELIA DANIELS

I.

SIX MONTHS BEFORE the end of the world, I start exchanging glances with the woman who holds the moon.

Not the woman *in* the moon, mind you. The woman just behind her, the one who gathers up the darkness every night and wears it as a veil. She's not much of a talker, not like her bright-blooded companion. But I'm still walking home from work in the dark, these days, and she is…approachable, in a way that the bright lights and waning tides are not.

It takes her a while to catch me looking—and why wouldn't it, when you have the moon in your arms?

And of course, I don't know the world's ending. Not yet. Looking back, I imagine the disaster of it all must have been more than a little distracting, from her perspective.

(But then again, what does that say about me, if I was able to get her attention?)

II.

THREE MONTHS BEFORE the end of the world, I start sending texts to the woman who holds the moon. The seas are rising, I explain, and can she please tell her girlfriend to ease up a little?

I get back a string of emojis I can't decipher, but it is... something.

So I keep texting her.

I send her exclamation points when Mississippi gives in to the water, and she sends me frowns in return. When I go on an ill-advised date with an ex before the last of the museums close, I whine to her all the way through—because why can't this idiot see that the sky-scraping circle of radios is actually a modern-day Tower of Babel? What does my date mean, saying that we have better things to do than listen to sound waves pop and fizz?

When the power starts to go out, the woman who holds the moon finally responds with something that isn't an emoji.

She tells me not to stop.

So she is the last person I text before my phone battery dies. I send her a photo of the big flowerpot in my kitchen, the ones with the peonies that just bloomed.

They burn when sparks fly out of my fuse box—but the apartment smells like the edge of summer for at least a week afterward.

III.

A MONTH BEFORE the end of the world, I start having coffee with the woman who holds the moon.

There aren't coffee shops open anymore, so she provides the brew. It tastes just a shade off, like it's been kept too long. I don't say anything, but she laughs when I wrinkle my nose and tells me that she's borrowed some of the ISS's supply. I ask if they won't miss it, but she only smiles in answer.

The moon joins us, now and again. She insists that I try all manner of blends—and her cabinet is immense. In that last month, I have coffee from a dozen different countries, some I can't even place on a map.

It's over those cups that the woman who holds the moon introduces me to her perspective. It isn't just Earth, after all, that she gets to see. She is as at home with our satellites as she is with our galactic neighbors'; she watches the storms on Jupiter even while she is here, making constellations in a coffee mug.

She sees the water rising and the fires just outside of town—but she doesn't tell me about those things. No—on the best days, when the moon sits in her lap and makes her darkness all the darker, she tells me about fields of flowers blooming in the Arctic. The pinks go on for miles, she says, they threaten to crawl up dying tree trunks just to find a place to stake their roots.

It sounds beautiful, I tell her, in between sips—and I try not to think about what it all implies.

IV.

TWO WEEKS BEFORE the end of the world, I start racing with the woman who holds the moon.

She's a fast runner, let me tell you. I leave behind everything in my little apartment, but even then, I can't keep up.

We still meet for coffee, of course, and the moon laughs at us both. But as the days get longer—and hotter, and brighter—it gets harder to make the time. In the few hours that we have together, I am exhausted from running.

The two of them run their fingers through my hair and heal where sunburn has started to peel my scalp away.

The woman who holds the moon asks me, as the days tick down, what it is I'm running for.

And I tell her. I'm honest. The moon joins her as she looks at me, my heart and soul on my tongue. I watch them take each other's hands—and it doesn't hurt, not like I thought it would.

It is impossible, I think, not to love the woman who holds the moon. Not to love the moon herself. Not at the end of days. It's—good, like the last sip of coffee on a cool and dark morning.

Like the rush of a forest fire, sparking just beyond the horizon.

Inevitable, really.

V.

A DAY BEFORE the end of the world, I say a prayer to the woman who holds the moon.

Standing in what was once Midwest suburbia, I ask her to forgive the coffee cups I've left in her sink. To forgive the peonies I left at home. I ask her to take those seeds in their pots and to sow them when I can't any longer. In a moment of selfishness, I ask her to take away my sunburn.

VI.

MINUTES BEFORE THE end of the world, I exchange a glance with the woman who holds the moon.

And she *smiles*.

(And the world still burns—but she's waiting for me in the darkness, her and her cool embrace.)

Sunshine City

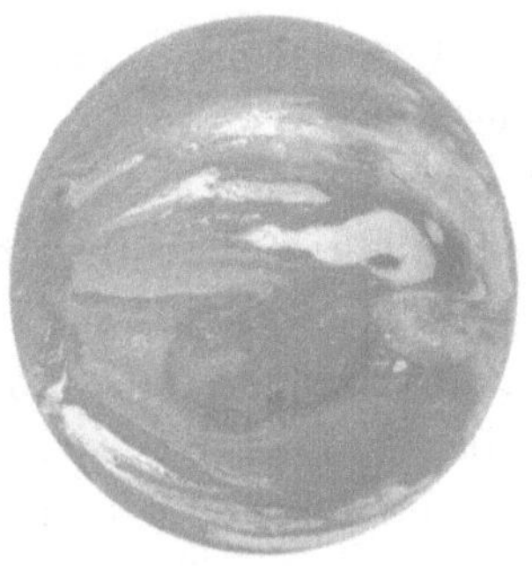

Catherine Yu

IZZY PROMISED WE were going to rule Sunshine City forever, but she turned out to be a liar.

The day she walked out for good, instead of overalls she wore a neat, pleated blue skirt I'd never seen before, paired with a white button-down shirt she'd once claimed to hate. The necklace around her neck was gone, leaving me dangling with the other half.

I thought she'd be back in a few minutes, or a few days at most. But the doors to Sunshine City were a one-way exit. I stayed behind, surrounded by glass castles and flushed clouds. I could hear the echo of her laughter, ringing like music.

I avoided my parents' questions for as long as I could manage. *Izzy was sick, Izzy was busy.* The lies made everything worse until they wised up and stopped asking altogether. But not before the gnawing started—little stirrings in my stomach.

A thin white strand poked through my shirt right in the middle of Geometry class. I tugged and it curled in my hand, small and singular. Harmless, maybe. The color reminded me of Izzy, thin and pale like an uncooked vermicelli noodle.

I had to do something hard that used to be so easy—I had to speak to her.

I saw her in the hallway with Sophia, arm-in-arm and laughing. I ducked into the girl's bathroom. I got into the last stall, the one no one ever used because it was haunted. I felt those slight pains again, and this time, I pulled out at least four from under my shirt. Little translucent threads that wriggled before finally lying flat and dead. I flushed them down the toilet.

I got my courage up to face Izzy after school, even though she was with not just Sophia now, but Ava and Taylor too. "Why won't you meet me *there* anymore?"

Her new friends laughed and my cheeks burned. Izzy looked away, like she was embarrassed to be around me. The other half of the necklace was still around my neck. I tore it off, flung it onto the grass, and sat as far from them as I could on the school bus home, my hands clutched over my stomach the whole ride.

That night, the threads got so bad that I got a pair of tweezers from Mom's vanity. In the privacy of my locked room, I plucked wriggling pieces one by one, gritting my teeth so I wouldn't make any noise. I wiped the blood on my sheets and threw the curdled dead things out the window. In the morning, Mom took one look at the mess I'd made of the sheets and handed me a pink feminine hygiene pad.

"You're becoming a woman," she said, her voice warm with pride.

I couldn't explain to her that it wasn't like that; this was something different.

I spent most of English the next morning in the girls'

bathroom. I pulled out so many threads that I almost fainted. I slid down the side of the cold wall and stared at the wriggling ball of pale threads in my hands, until they eventually stopped moving.

If it kept going like this, I'd be dead in a matter of days. The bleeding was getting worse, seeping through my clothes and getting harder to hide, even with my coat wrapped around me tight. A hall monitor found me curled up on the floor and sent me home immediately.

"This is what becoming a woman is about," Mom said.

Under the blanket, the threads were coming out and crawling over my body. "This is perfectly normal," she reiterated. "It's okay to grow apart from friends, too. It happens to everyone at some point."

"It's *not* about Izzy," I managed to say. I felt like a thread was squeezing around my heart, trying to poke in instead of out.

"Then what is this about?" she asked.

I never did figure out how to explain it to her.

†

Twenty years later, Stella and I were moving in together for the first time. We loaded cardboard boxes of our separate possessions and unloaded them into our new apartment, a small studio space in South Brooklyn. We unpacked everything indiscriminately of who they belonged to. Inside one box, I found a lacquered enamel box filled with jade bracelets and gold hoop earrings— and a necklace, too. Half a tarnished-silver heart, *Best* inscribed onto it.

It brought me right back to Sunshine City. The phantom threads began moving in my stomach, even though so much time had passed. I breathed in and out, dispelling visions of the past…but the ache still lingered. The iridescent mirrors and fantastical glimpses of elsewhere melded back into the silver necklace in my hand, an orange cascade of afternoon light spilling in from the open window.

My girlfriend came over and rested her chin on my shoulder. "It's hard for me to get rid of old things," she mumbled against my hair. "I must've had that one for years. Got it with my best friend at summer camp when we were kids."

Sunshine City only had room for two of us, until suddenly it didn't. Izzy left it first, but I'd followed shortly after. There was no point in ruling it alone. It made me sad. Even now, in the new apartment I shared with the person I loved most.

Would she think it was a foolish thing to reminisce about, so many years later? But by the time I finished my story, she looked at me thoughtfully, and I knew she was taking what I'd said quite seriously.

"Aren't we there right now? Or couldn't we be close?" she asked.

I looked at the cardboard boxes around us, the shelves lined with our collective books. I looked at the sun-warmed wood beams of our small apartment. I looked at her, the woman squeezing my hand. There was a smudge of dirt on her cheek from unpacking. I brushed it away with the soft pad of my thumb. "Yeah," I said, as surprised as I was sure of it. "Of course we are."

The tea kettle whistled in the kitchen. I got up to check, and Stella followed.

Flammable Contents

Tessa Fisher

They strip us, first. They strip us of everything—our clothing, our belongings, our names, even our hometowns. We vanish from the official records, just some anonymous naked human bodies kept in cells.

Who *they* are, what they call themselves, that doesn't matter, not really. I find a little solace in knowing their days are numbered—their ideology requires the existence of enemies to function, and sooner or later, they'll run out of easy prey, and either pick a fight someone can't beat, or turn on each other. Fascism, after all, is still a suicide cult at the end of the day. The fire that sustains it will always burn itself out.

They don't intend to kill us—they've made that much clear. Knowing what they're going to do instead, I find this deeply unfortunate.

†

THE EARLIEST REPORTED case of spontaneous human combustion was written about in 1613. The victim, one John Hitchell, was found burned to death in his bed by his wife; a pamphlet about the strange event called it "fire from heaven." That description would set the pattern for most accounts of the phenomenon throughout the following centuries: victim's flesh and bone burned down to ash, but the surrounding area oddly undamaged. I always thought it sounded underwhelming—if I had to burn to death, I at least wanted the consolation of not burning alone.

†

THEY SHOW US a few of the women who came before us—their chests scarred, their genitals maimed. I suspect they intend to inflict the latter on me—they have neither the skill nor the desire to try to reassemble my penis, and will likely just crudely erase my womanhood and be done with it. I'm not sure what they do with the trans men that weren't lucky enough to escape, but it's probably best not something dwelled upon.

They tell us they're "restoring the masculinity that was unjustly taken by an overly permissive society," making us "true men" again. We're supposed to be grateful. At first, I wonder why they simply don't kill us, as has been the preferred course of action for most fascist regimes when confronting the offensive existence of the transfeminine, until I learn they intend to use us as a source of labor, too bereft and broken to fight back.

But they don't seem to realize that there's nothing more volatile than someone who has nothing left to lose.

†

THE MOST LIKELY cause of spontaneous human combustion is fairly mundane: the victim accidentally ignites their clothing, via sparks from a fireplace, or a carelessly placed cigarette. Quickly succumbing to the conflagration, the fat from the victim's body begins to liquefy, and is drawn into the victim's clothing—the so-called "wick effect"—which sustains the fire for hours, long enough to thoroughly cremate the remains. The fire burns at low temperature, and is limited in its ability to spread laterally, explaining the lack of damage in the surroundings.

This theory would also explain why spontaneous human combustion seemed to strike the elderly, who might be less able to extinguish their burning clothing, and smokers and alcoholics in particular. Oddly, women were disproportionately represented in the case files, to the point that in the Victorian era, it was believed that only women were subject to such a fate.

†

THE CELLS ARE sterile but cold. We shiver and huddle together for warmth, telling each other our names—our true names, not the ones our captors insist on calling us— to remind ourselves of who we really are.

(Often, they aren't able to find records of our deadnames, so they call us a masculinized version of our chosen names. This gives me a small bit of amusement; my deadname was nothing at all like my chosen name).

In college I took a course in Buddhism, where there was a brief discussion of the Tibetan meditative practice of tummo. Using biofeedback and breathing techniques, monks engaged in tummo could raise their body temperatures at will to an extraordinary degree. Some even made a game of it, standing outside in the Himalayan winter and throwing wet robes on each other, seeing who could evaporate the most water, steam rising from their bodies. I wish I could have learned this art back then—but novice practitioners are discouraged from learning tummo, out of concern that they could seriously hurt themselves in the process.

†

THE WICK EFFECT isn't the only theory that's been put forward for spontaneous human combustion. The Victorians blamed alcohol, and assumed victims were drunkards so saturated with flammable spirits that it was only a matter of time before they went flambé. Others suggested ball lightning.

Larry Arnold, in his 1995 book *Ablaze*, suggested multiple theories: that such incidents were the result of a particular confluence of ley lines; that it was caused by a hitherto-unknown quantum particle he dubbed a "pyrotron" that sparked an "internal Hiroshima" within the victims' bodies; or, invoking kundalini yoga traditions similar to tummo, that extreme emotional stress itself was enough to trigger combustion. I always found this last one the most interesting—perhaps it was why women seemed to be more often affected.

†

THEY PICK ME up and pull me out of the cell. Not without a fight—I struggle as hard as I can, and I think I manage to give one of them a bloody nose at least. They beat me, of course, but my skin is so numb from the cold that the pain is almost a nice change of pace.

They drag me to the would-be operating room they've set up, my limbs flailing. I consider a break for freedom, only for them to strap me onto a table.

They slip a breathing mask on my face and a subtle metallic perfume of nitrous oxide tickles my nose. I breathe shallow and fast, partially out of fear, and partially out of a stubborn desire not to let them take my consciousness from me too. I want to bear witness to this horror. I'm hot and sweaty, my muscles quivering.

The two putative surgeons hover over me, their hands ready. A fire here could do some good—could burn those surgeons' hands, wreck their instruments. Maybe it could even cause some real destruction if one of the oxygen tanks goes up, to spare my sisters this horrific mutilation. It would mean my death, but I accepted that fate the moment two thugs jumped me outside my apartment door, and hauled me off to the cells.

My breathing grows faster as the surgeons finish their preparations, and I float in and out of consciousness. A ball of heat burns within me—a ball of hatred, of righteous anger, of sorrow for those who came before me and those that might come after. I fan it as best I can.

Perhaps my name will be remembered for centuries, like John Hitchell, despite the best efforts of these monstrous fools. Or perhaps it, too, will be consumed by the fire.

The sharp bite of the scalpel sinks into my left breast, and I ignite.

God Daughter's Shanty

Sydney Sackett

M Y FATHER WAS only a ruddy-faced fisherman's whelp when the ocean goddess emerged before him, all streaming dark hair and garlands of corroded netting and pearls. He knelt to her, respect learned under a stiff hand at his family's driftwood shrine. It pleased her when he ran here and there for her careless orders, fetching first a nosegay of gull feathers and pink geraniums and horned yellow poppies, next building her a throne of sand twenty handspans high. He hunted a week for a blue crab that evaded him while she watched from her new perch, lip drawn between double rows of teeth.

In return, as she considered her right and his gift, the sea goddess caught his curls and dragged him deep to a stinging bed of anemone. The waves broke five times with her passion. Eventually, mouth salt-burned and bloody, he crawled back gasping on the beach. Her slick tentacles had squeezed the life from his left leg, and from then on it hung pale and fleshy, refusing to support him.

He got no farther than his doorstep. Rain washed him. The sun dried him in the morning. Silhouetted before the tempered water, the sand throne crumbled back to earth.

He said nothing when his father's boat returned. He only asked for a crutch to hold himself upright. He never joined the men who dared the waves in their wooden vessels, but he kept the house and salted the barrels of fish, and for a little while he hoped he could forget.

In nine months, I was delivered to him in a tide pool, with curls as bright as his and squalls as rowdy as a hurricane.

†

"Why won't my mother visit?" I complained to my father as a girl, drumming hungrily on the table. I would eat raw creatures whole, cracking into urchins and lobsters festooned with kelp. Whale oil had been my milk. I never understood his fear when I played in the shallows, laughing as I breathed water, or his pain when I shrieked and battered other children for their offenses. Soon it was only us two. Bored and lonely, I threw legendary tantrums, the thunder answering me for every howl.

In my sixteenth year, after he caught me kissing a mariner's girl under the pier, my ragged nails stripping her back, my father told me the story of the goddess who stole him away. Like draining ink from a stone came this secret he had endured. I wept so hard that clouds bloomed in the open sky for days on end. I paced along the water's edge and screamed at my mother. For the damage she had done. For how she'd forgotten. For never coming back to us.

I realized then I had to be the one to find her. So I began my hunt alone.

†

I soon discovered I wasn't the only one after all.

A man with the black and white wings of a great petrel was the first to join me. He'd been living in a tent, covered in his own shit and mud, eating rotten meat thrown to him by bored sailors. He never knew his mother either, whom he'd killed thrashing free of her belly with his talons, or the father who had flown to her bed at the sight of her shiny locket. I washed that broken man clean in the tide. And following the tale of her wild charms, we found the bard's daughter, who'd grown in her mother from nothing more than a song. Her shanties stirred courage into the softest hearts. By that time, from every corner of the coast, the gods' children were coming to *us*.

We took in the old man born from a turtle's egg, the dangerous woman whose mother was struck by living lightning, and the polar boy who hoped to rescue his father from a grotto of frozen trophies. Siblings, too— some of us met strangers starred with the same curses. Two cloud-dragon brothers embracing and crying a fog that grounded all the ships in port. An outcast in a skin of sloughing algae who clasped her tiny sister's budding green hands like a rope thrown to save her life. I never did find one to match me. If my mother birthed other spawn, perhaps she kept them in her realm. In my weakest moments, that was the life I wished for. Pearls and shark teeth on strings, singing with a goddess to the backing of the storm, never answering to a mortal soul.

But I do answer to one. He walks on a cane and he is waiting for me to come home golden-handed with ichor.

†

LOVELY AND TERRIBLE, the daughter of the sun met me last. My Brightness. We'd taken her for a leper. Shrouded in black, she said the glow of her body could burn and disease. I was impetuous as weather—I asked to see her wholly, and she shrugged her cloak off in my quarters.

I would have taken more than sunburns to have that night again. So I did, and I did, and I did.

Together, we embarked. Behind us, the other children of the gods would guard our mortals. No more mortals raped and stolen for divine diversion. Instead our petrel man will take flight and raise the warning call, so the dragons and lightning woman can slake their rage. The bard will lead the turtle man and the glacial boy and many others with her melody to destroy the shrines that stand in human homes. And if my story will still be told, it'll be through her shanties too.

My Brightness and I sail to seek revenge at the horizon where the sea and sun cross. I bring nets and jars of lightning and knives of ice at the side of a girl who warms the bitter sea of me to mist. Before we kill our divines, we will show them that we found the kind of love they can never understand.

The hot blood in me is stronger than my mother's cruel salt water: I learned the best of my tricks from the fishermen who tamed her all their lives. To drag her carcass finally ashore can only be our right, and, gods help her, we could have no greater gift.

Haus Lobo

Malik Berry

For Lula, the Realness category was the best part of
the ball. Something about seeing all her friends put
on the front of playing straight tickled her. It was also
the category Lula slayed on a regular basis.

All the children came through looking gorgeous, earlier
than everyone but the judges; they wanted to stunt on
everybody there. One of the biggest mistakes they made
was dolling up too much. There's a big difference between
a look and a get-up. The kids always ended up wearing
get-ups. You saw the costume before you saw the person.
It's fine if you're judging how creative they got, but for
Realness, you needed to prove you could move through the
straight world without clocking anyone's radar.

Earlier in the night, Lula stunted in Chanel cocktail
dresses she bought from Goodwill. Then she appeared in
a sequin gown and gloves, doing her best Jessica Rabbit
strut and sashay. No eyes in the house weren't bulging
like a cartoon, and no fingers weren't snapping in ecstatic
approval. She killed it without any argument, from the

judges or the rest of the house children, but she was just getting started. Lula brought the house down on Realness. She was so good, no one else should even try.

The routine began the same every time. All the lights went out, except for a single floor lamp in the center of the ball with a red sash over it. While regulars cheered and hollered, the new blood looked around in anticipation. After a while, anticipation became annoyance. Lula loved to make them wait.

Even longer, annoyance would grow into dread. Lula loved to see them squirm. At the peak of the tension, a foot stepped into the small circle of light on the wooden floor, but it wore no pump, clog, or loafer. No skin either. The foot was a massive brown-furred paw, nails painted red. It appeared disembodied in the darkness, until it was followed by another painted paw, this one grabbing the stem of the lamp like a dancer's pole. She pulled the sash off, the light of the unshaded bulb pouring over her true face, the elongated visage of a wolf. Somehow still elegant, even with teeth as long as blades, her eyes were lit with fiery feral pupils. At six feet without pumps, Lula was already tall in human form. Now she towered a foot beneath the unreflecting disco ball.

Some gasped but the newcomers didn't scream. They'd been marked, and they knew what they'd signed up for.

All were silent as Lula scanned the crowd, the illuminated eyes of her regulars staring back at her. Confident as she was, Lula still dreaded this moment. The ball was meant to be a refuge from the pain in the straight world, but as years went on, it just became another hunting ground. Not every regular had good judgment— some might have invited interlopers who saw them as a freakshow to be gawked at. Or worse, they could turn violent, and with a purpose. Lula had lost friends to silver daggers from these invasions. She lost more to silver bullets on the streets when someone clocked them.

Her enhanced vision scanned the dark room, watching for any movement from the newcomers. She sniffed the air, and only her family's familiar scent filled her nostrils, setting her nerves at rest. Dozens more glowing eyes appeared in the dark before the lights slowly turned back on, dimmer than ever. No longer drawing attention to themselves with tacky get-ups, the newcomers began shedding their skin, revealing new grown fur and elongated limbs as more than comfortable enough for them. Soon they'd learn how to become the kind of prey that didn't go down without a fight.

"And so concludes the initiation of Haus Lobo," Lula announced in her booming voice. "Now make your mother proud."

The congregation howled in reply, and out they went into the streets, to slay and rend all who threaten the fiercest creatures of the night.

BY ANY OTHER NAME

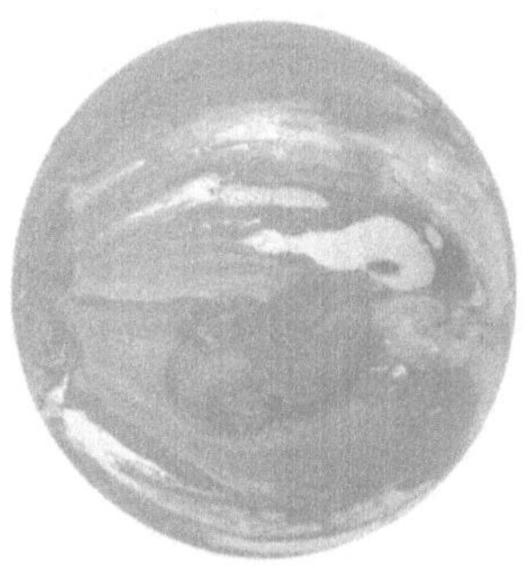

BRIE ATIENZA

CRAVING COMES WITH the desire. Tangled as they are, it feels odd to envision them as separate, but one is concentrated in the stomach and salivary glands, and the other starts in the heart and radiates into a full-body experience. Both refuse to cease with a liter of cold water and logic. Both are a type of ache.

At breakfast I masticate damp petals into mush. Nutty daisies mingle with the gentle piquancy of lilies, peppered with sweet clouds of baby's breath. At dinner I dine on supermarket stalks and snack on little flowers plucked from pavement cracks.

You text me a photo of the bouquet and bonbons delivered to your door, asking, The hell is this?

My bowl is empty but my stomach growls anew at the sight of juicy bright petals and crispy green leaves, freshly misted—

Excitement triggers a coughing fit. Spit spatters the tabletop. I heave petals back into the bowl. They're warm and pink, like my cheeks at your name. Not yet scarlet.

I reply, *Just thinking of you.*

†

EARLY REPORTS ASSUMED the flowers bloomed from the heart and spread to other organs. Victims were found facedown in pools of bloody petals, mouths stuffed, pistils and stamens extracted from the stomach and lungs. As research progressed and fatalities decreased, we learned. Hanaueru doesn't bloom within a body filled with casual love; it isn't that kind. It's consumption and starvation. We are complicit in our own destruction.

†

YOUR KEY CLICKS in the lock, and you enter, radiant with sweat. I wave you to my dining table, still plucking flower heads. I pop fistfuls like potato chips. Yesterday I stopped using cutlery; it's an unnecessary step between my mouth and the flowers.

"Woah, hey, slow down." Your favorite chair screeches. "Did you…meet someone?" Hope springs eternal. Obviously I'm eating raw flowers, but the bouquet could've been celebratory, or a morbid joke.

I wipe my mouth with a sleeve, and a dollop of red smears against my wrist. "No."

You can't bear to see the bloody spit or the decapitated stems. You can't meet my eyes, either. I understand why—I am searching without intending to scour. A part of me has germinated and screams for a garden only you can water. It's embarrassing.

"How long?" you ask.

You mean the flower-craving? A month, since the first vague hankering. You mean, the feeling—or, rather, the not-quite-and-beyond feeling, the state of being? I don't know. There was an inkling, as early as the first time we spoke under a sunrise. Growing over nights spent on the same bed. Blooming when hands brushed as we swiveled on barstools.

"Don't talk with your mouth full." You chide dab at my chin with a napkin; the same thing you said as we shared crackers on a bus ride to the planetarium. You smile at me, then frown at the napkin. Petals are plastered to the wet paper, purple and pink and red.

How to give words to the desire as I'm hounded by the craving? I try: "I want to spend the rest of my life with you."

"We're already gonna do that," you say. "Provided you don't die of malnutrition or, like, pesticide poisoning."

I reach for a rose. "You know what I mean."

"No, I don't."

Slow down, you told me. I tear the petals one at a time, alternating words in my head: *Loves me, loves me not,* a chant to change the impending disaster. My throat hurts. It's getting harder to chew.

A petal slips from my grip, and falls and flits in front of you. You pinch it between thumb and index finger, wrinkles forming around your inquisitive gaze. My heart leaps as you nibble the petal's edge. I ache at the movement of your lips. I can't read your expression.

You swallow. Immediately your jaw spasms, your cheeks. Your throat bobs. You hack and hack and retch. The eviscerated petal splats onto the tablecloth.

"No," you choke out, confirming, "I don't know."

Is a rose still a rose when all its petals are gone? The last tears away on a not, tastes of ash on my tongue. I will be gracious and noble even if I'm doomed.

You bite your lip till it's swollen. "Do you think it'll pass?"

I pretend to consider it. "No."

†

WHEN YOU RETURN, bald stems litter the table and dirty flower water dries on the floor and I'm sniffling, sitting in your chair. It's wobbly from uneven legs, but you like it this way, insist it isn't broken.

You spread a brochure in front of me. It's cream-and-blue, soothing. I catch the words *surgery, life-saving.*

"No," I say, firmly, crumpling the brochure. "I don't want to stop loving you."

"So you'd rather die?" Your lips curl like thorns. "How's that supposed to make me feel?"

"Horrified, I'd imagine." I smile weakly. "And flattered?" I would die for you — even because of you. Do you understand? I would let you kill me.

Your eyes are shining with unshed tears. I catch my breath.

"I'm sorry," I say. "I ruined everything. I made things weird."

"Shush," you say. "Nothing's ruined. Sure, it's weird, but everything's weird these days. Even the surgery is weird." The brochure is wrinkled and creased at every angle; you must've read it many times. "See? Turns out it isn't a removal…"

I can't see where you're pointing through the tears. My chest constricts, a rabbit-thump heartbeat like thunder and lightning, harder when you pull me against your own. I close my eyes and inhale the scent of your shampoo. I'll think about it, I promise, after I stop thinking about knowing I'm dying.

†

I OPEN MY eyes, and it's the dead of night, lights-off, but I can see. A white-framed window. A privacy curtain. You, asleep upright in an armchair, pulled close to my bed.

My head and chest itch. I'm thirsty, and hungry for real food. In other words, I don't feel nothing. When you wake, there will be a crick in your neck, a joyful reunion, some residual awkwardness. Right now, I spot a bouquet lopsided on the bedside table, a small box of candy hearts, and a card made of pink construction paper where you—definitely you—have scribbled: *Get well soon! Love you.*

I touch my lips, my stomach. The scars will be the only evidence of desire, rewired or relocated. I touch my throat—it's mostly painless, my pulse steady. I take another look at you, then at the card. With some effort, I can smile. I still have what I need.

Notes on Genocidal Interchronological Incursion 57.7.3 (F.K.A. "Friends")

Sam J. Miller

First RULE OF forgery detection: time is the best investigator. Distance lets us see clearly the patterns we missed up close. Forgers exploit the ignorance of their audience, and optimize their frauds to the biases and misunderstandings of the moment. Look at what passed for a Ming Dynasty vase in the 19th century New York art market and you'll laugh out loud.

To say nothing of new technologies. Carbon dating, X-ray fluorescence, gas chromatography mass spectrometry...they all pull away the wool that covered the eyes of previous generations.

So what seems obvious to us now, knowing what we do, was completely missed by our antecedents and ancestors.

We must forgive them. How could they have known? Their imagination and their capacity for meaningful action were dramatically smaller than they believed them to be. As are our own.

Late 20th-century American audiences for serialized narratives physically broadcast through terrestrial signal transmission (fka "television") had no reason to suspect that the stories they consumed came from anywhere other than their own time and space; between corporate control of telecommunications channels and historic legacies of exploitation and oppression there was more than enough evil to explain away any toxic agenda detected inside the content of their beloved "shows."

Because in the 1990s, the development of interchronological data transmission technologies was still seventy years away. The ability to send signals back in time was the stuff of science fiction...and in our ancestors' fantasies, the future usually sent back killer robots instead of banal packets of data in the form of emails and text messages with instructions to human agents to set up shell companies, invest in specific stocks, accrue capital, carry out insidious schemes.

These schemes were blunt instruments. Their vast impacts far exceeded their intended outcomes, eagerly burning down entire forest to kill small specific trees. And there were so many forest fires. Every day, it seems, interchronological forensics unmasks a new inferno.

Today, in this dossier, we are revealing one such scheme, concerning real estate market manipulation in Node Nine of the Circumatlantic Urban Agglomeration (f.k.a. "The Elbow;" f.f.k.a. "New York City").

In the 1980s, government action in the release of freebased cocaine hydrochloride ("crack") and inaction in the spread of the Human Immunodeficiency Virus caused Node Nine to become economically unstable. Property values plummeted. The wealthy fled en masse. Its perception in the popular imagination was of a dangerous collapsing crime-ridden hellhole. A prison to be escaped from.

Other forensics experts have exposed many of the ugly interchronological interventions that Node Nine slumlords in our own time have deployed with the intent of changing the past and shifting that perception in order to increase the value of their assets and holdings. Foremost among these are the transformation of "Times Square" from sex worker safe space to expensive Disney World satellite, and the "Broken Windows" theory of policing—advanced by an insidious think tank long since proven to be exclusively a mouthpiece for toxic fascists from the future—which held that aggressive widespread police abuse of low-income communities of color would boost tourism.

What has gone undocumented—until *this* document—is recognition of the "television" "show" *Friends* as an additional interchronological incursion, one intended to overwrite the city's chaotic colorful reality with one scrubbed clean of all the things that made life there special, and markets unpredictable.

Seeing the show now, it's hard to appreciate the transformation it achieved. How little it looked like the place it was purporting to represent.

Racial diversity, seen as economically undesirable, was erased. So was class struggle and street art and the dire magnificent pluropotentiality of sex and violence and love and creativity that throbbed inside of every fraught random interaction on the sidewalks and subways and piers and clubs and playgrounds.

New York viewers of the 1990s and 2000s laughed at the ridiculousness of the program's representation of their city, but they were not the show's intended audience. Nor were the contemporary suburbanites who made up its main viewership in the era of its airing.

No, the show was meant for their children. The ones who saw it out of the corner of their eyes as they grew up, and for whom it formed the primary image of what

New York City was. The ones who saw not a crime-ridden hellhole, but a safe bland warm-and-fuzzy place where they could hang out with other people who looked just like them. The ones who would soon grow up, and start moving to New York en masse. Driving up prices. Pushing people out. Replacing grubby bodegas with airy monochromatic coffee shops, their names nowhere near as clever as they imagined.

Only in the coming decades, as this nightmare vision of a sanitized soulless New York City came to become the reality, did the pattern become clear. The forgery became apparent. By the late 2010s, it was often impossible to tell the difference. Stand on certain street corners in certain neighborhoods—once overwhelmingly working-class—and you'd see nothing but an unending stream of soullessly attractive gentrifiers. The grotesque proliferation of Friends merchandise in the 2020s was an added insult from the future, a slap in the face to say: *Look. Look around you. Look what we've done. You laughed at this show, and now this show laughs at you.*

Attached, you'll find full forensics. The communiques from known transchronological front companies, instructing terrestrial transmission content creation mills in what to write, who to cast, how to market. The fingerprints are clear.

You may well ask, like my mother, like many of my peers: what does it matter? The show has vanished into the void of history. Neither the city nor the nation that Node Nine once belonged to still exists. The damage is done; the tree is burned down. Why bother to figure out how?

And I'd have had an answer for you years ago, when I first started my studies in interchronological forensics. I'd have had a prepared rant ready to roll, about how understanding the atrocities of the past allows us to prevent future nefariousnesses. I'd have delivered it with a straight face. I'd have believed it.

But here's the thing. Time is the best investigator, but time is also every criminal's accomplice. While it does its slow work, the guilty live good lives, grow old, die, bequeath their bloody spoils to innocent children.

And so the ancient adage turns out to be true: we who remember the past are doomed to repeat it.

A Demon Dates in New York City

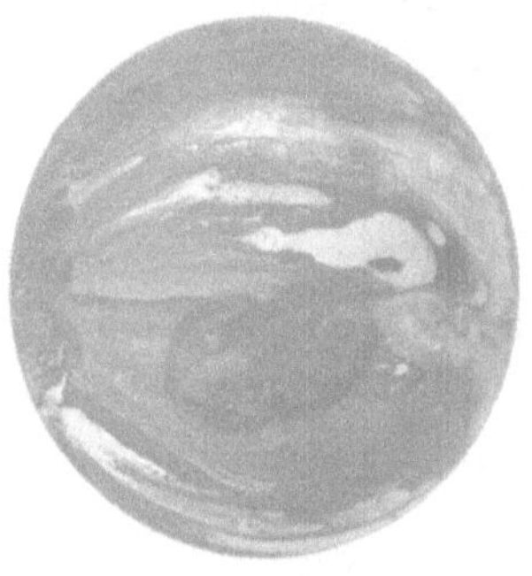

JARED POVANDA

IMITRI DIED IN 1792, and still I grieved. Sometimes this grief was a scrim of murk, algae obscuring a pond flat with reflection. Other times, grief was pellucid light through clean water at a farm upstate, an intentional offering to the bright flare of his memory.

The world, when we met, was hard for men like us. Dimitri had to secret me up to his cluttered attic room above the print shop, and he was always tired, always covered in smoke and sweat. It was hot in the attic. It was better without clothes. I loved kissing his closed eyes before I kissed his mouth—a sort of prayer, taboo for my kind—amidst masculine shouts and the press grinding below. I would meander over his body like a stream, mouth drifting along skin. Dimitri died young. At the end, I sat by his bedside and pressed one damp rag after another to his fevered head. Air rattled through his weak lungs, and over the following years, I winced whenever I heard winter-bare branches tapping glass.

Different scents and sounds permeated in 2023, but I still found myself wanting to be a river for the men I found myself with—*flow through me, let me give you back to yourself.* Last night, I went on a date with a witch from Manhattan. While he spoke about a trip to Taiwan, his folded napkin grew legs and tried to walk off the table. I caught it before it could escape. We laughed. We shared dessert.

Inside his apartment, hyacinths pulsed in time with our heartbeats. Leaves in the shapes of birds fluttered shadows across the ceiling. It was an aerie, an aquarium of air. Tail around his wrist, his lips at my horns, and when he kissed one of their sharp points, I marveled at the gentleness existent in this world.

In the morning, I made us coffee and said goodbye. I longed to run my hands through his curls, to feel the continual delight of his unhorned scalp, but even after hundreds of years, newness frightened me, made me hesitant to push too hard.

Instead, I left to water my own plants. I couldn't compete with a witch in an open concept loft, but I liked to try to keep things alive. Water rained over green leaves, honeysuckle, and then into black soil.

As lunar moths curved in my stomach, reminding me of first times with other men I'd kissed and ached for through wars and decades and lives, Dimitri was still the wall behind the climbing ivy, my foundation. Even when he could no longer speak, he refused to drop my hand. I let the can levitate, pulled out my phone, and typed: *Thank you for last night.*

As I moved into the kitchen to warm a corn muffin in the oven, I felt pearl and gleaming, a cup of gilded milk.

Gray bubbles on my screen meant clear water—cold bathing with phlox crowning the banks. It meant he was texting me back.

A Spell Forgotten

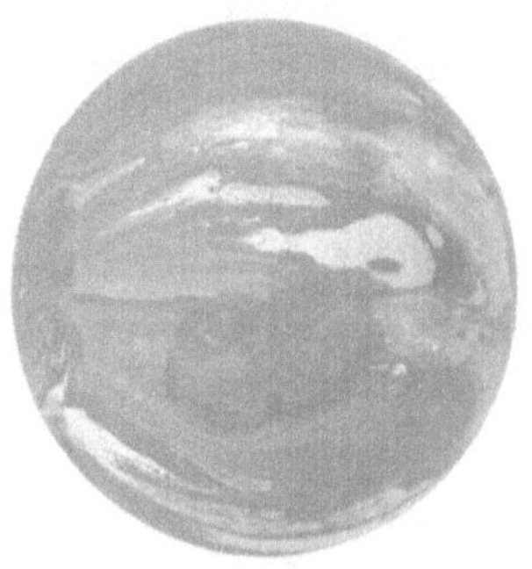

P. H. Low

IT IS YOUR fault, they say, when you lose your magic. In the land where you are born, it was outlawed until recently. Your parents still speak of it in hushed tones, only ward the living room when they think you're asleep. At two years old, you blossom your mother's houseplants with a touch, as infants are wont to do, but then you're shunted off to preschool and forget. You grow up with sidelong glances and teachers who do not look you in the face, grow up watching non-magical classmates pull up the corners of their eyes and run away from you during recess. No letter on cream-colored parchment comes when you turn ten or twelve, inviting you back to an old-country academy to nurture your latent abilities; no encyclopedic knowledge of runes lights up your brain upon puberty. Alone in your bedroom, you pinch your fingers, trying to coax out sparks, and wonder if your parents could have at least taught you the social rules of non-magicals instead.

When you grow older, you try everything to get it back. Short of returning, of course—it is a treacherous country for those without defense-spells sparking at their palms, those who cannot shield themself from the onslaught of that which they do not know. You attend university—non-magical, again—and, around the crushing weight of your engineering major, memorize a few wars your country has won, learn the way unused neurons are pruned from infants' brains, and how they stop hearing entire ranges of phonemes because their systems deem them irrelevant.

Your magic is gone, your professors tell you, though never in those words. *You'll never get it back.*

And it's your fault.

You graduate, in time. Move to a bright new city where you can pretend you've lost nothing. You work and drink and pay rent that's too damn high, and when you lie alone at night, you tell yourself this is the best life you can have.

Then one evening, as you walk home from the office under a cold grey sky, you pass a rune scratched on an open door.

You hesitate, shove your fists in your pockets. *Just vandalism,* you tell yourself. *These could be all over the city.* But the sweet milky ozone-scent of magic wafts from the stairs below, and an ache echoes in your chest: like the heartbeat after you've been shot, as you realize you are hemorrhaging blood.

You follow the stairs down.

A dark, crowded basement, a person with eyes like yours perched on a barstool. They're telling a story of your parents' homeland—a contentious election, the sly interference of the country you live in now. The speaker is much younger than you, and as they career into a digression, citing sources and explaining various scholars' takes, you feel a twinge of regret, that you lacked the energy or curiosity to read between the lines of your gen eds. Perhaps you could have had this, been this, if you'd wanted it a little more. But you're a worker, now—your time for transcendence has passed.

You return the next week, and the weeks after that. It is not always the same person regaling the bar with forgotten histories: there is an eyebrow-pierced woman in a leather jacket; a man wearing scrubs, having rushed straight from the hospital. But the nights belonging to the first storyteller are your favorite, crackling with fire and indignation. They tell of all the ways your country has mangled that of your parents'—the stoked racial divisions and causeless wars, the forests ashed to fuel its bottomless appetite. You learn about the hangings, the refusals to pay wages, the neighborhoods set on fire, and you want to weep, you want to break the world.

On a night in which you are feeling particularly fragile—in which they have spoken of students burning a religious school, hands flared bright with illicit magic as police shot them down—the storyteller leaves the stage afterward, sits beside you at the bar. As holiday music crescendos around you, your gaze skates along the rolled-up sleeves of their button-down, the dark hair falling in their eyes.

Warmth pools in your stomach, despite the weight of newfound history.

I see you around a lot, they say. *Are you a mage?*

To your mortification, your eyes well with tears.

Sorry, you say, awkwardly wiping your face. *I used to be. But it's gone, now. And I always thought I hadn't tried hard enough to learn, but—*

The residue of decades past still ripples the air between you: spellwork blazed from hands that should have been soft and helpless; the policemen's bloodshot eyes full of fear. *I'd never felt, before, like it wasn't my fault.*

The storyteller takes the drink the bartender offers them, sips thoughtfully. *You're learning that empire is built on violence.*

You gulp your own wine, feel yourself uncouth. In the low light, their eyes are nearly the same color as yours. *Yeah.*

And that it will continue to be, no matter what its own law says. Your laugh comes out watery. *Yeah.*

A perturbation crosses their face, a brief darkness like cloud-shadow. *It is not your fault,* they say softly. *This weight is not yours to bear alone.*

And then you are crying in earnest and they open their arms and by some deep-buried instinct you fall into them—trying to speak, to flatten your hurt into language—and they hold you and pat your shoulder and whisper, *darling, darling. I'm so sorry about what they've done.*

If You Lingered

Matt Richardson

IF YOU WANTED medicine, the kind that village doctors wouldn't provide, the kind made only with rare magic, then a wary local might guide you to a door in a nondescript alleyway. Squished between a pub and a cobbler, visitors to the town often missed it, but the locals knew exactly how to find it and exactly who owned it.

Albert's Apothecary—plain in name but not in wares—was run by a man named Thomas, son of the late Albert and a far better apothecary than his father ever dreamed of being. A better apothecary he may be, but a better man he was not, according to the locals of the town.

There was nearly always a warning when you asked around town for such medicine. Thomas was the most impolite man they'd ever met, they'd say. He was known for his rudeness and would make awful comments about the state of one's clothing, if you bothered to ask the mayor's wife about him. But, they'd admit, he was good at what he did. Good at controlling old magic.

Rumours had surrounded Albert's Apothecary for longer than Thomas had been there. The daughter of the family had disappeared when she was a teenager. Gone in the night without a word. Most believed she had left to find a better use for her abilities than a cramped alleyway.

When Thomas arrived months later, a supposed bastard son already trained in the art of making medicine and ready to take up his father's mantle, the townsfolk whispered. That Thomas had killed the daughter, and decided to play at being family with Albert. Or that Albert had grown desperate after the loss of his daughter—anyone would take the kind of money he had. Some mentioned how similar the son looked to the daughter—almost identical, in fact—but they were drowned out by the cries of cruelty against such a young and dainty soul, that someone so vicious should take charge instead of her.

And yet, they went to him anyway. Because while the rumours were hideous and vile, Thomas was more skilled than most.

When you walked into the store, you'd always be treated to the same sight: dim lighting, shelves upon shelves of jars and herbs and overgrown plants, and a man at a counter, mixing substances together in one of many bowls. Thomas would take a moment to notice you, and wouldn't greet you the way a shopkeeper usually would. He'd wait until you spoke.

Thomas hummed as he worked, this strange man with a youthful face and jaded eyes, face in a permanent scowl. You might not notice the way he tapped at his wrists as he grumbled and growled, taking your order with the promise to deliver as soon as possible.

You might linger, stare at the jars and ask questions. If you got a response, it would be stilted and guarded, until he let fly with a flurry of explanation on plants and the way magic coursed through them. Perhaps you understand him, or perhaps he'd look at your confusion, glare, and turn back towards his work.

You'd leave the apothecary believing all the unpleasant rumours, but the vitality that coursed through your body when you drank his medicine would make it worth it. It always did.

Later, you'd join the rest of the townsfolk in their whispers, describing your encounter with the strangest man in town. The others would agree with you, tell their own exaggerated stories about the things he'd said to them. All would agree that they would never like to be around Thomas for longer than necessary, but they had never felt better in years.

If you happened to wait in the alley until the store closed, which no one ever did, you'd see Thomas slowly clean up the day's mess. He'd hum to himself again, not smiling but seemingly happy with his work. It would take him a little more than an hour, but he always looked calmer than he ever did when the apothecary was open.

Most days, if you waited long enough, another man would unlock the front door and step through. The apothecary's front window didn't provide much of a view, but if it did, you would see him approach Thomas with bags full of herbs and supplies. You might expect the man to turn and leave like everyone else, but he wouldn't. He never did.

If the view was good, if you cared enough about Thomas to linger and watch, you would see him smile in a way no one ever expected from him. You would see them share a kiss. Perhaps you run then and tell everyone of what you saw, spreading more and more rumours until the whole town forgot there was a person behind them.

But if you didn't, if you stayed, you would see them head upstairs to the home above the store. You'd hear Thomas rant about all the ways he could use the new herbs he'd been given. You'd see the man smile, fond and gentle. You'd see Thomas reach for him, speak kindly, act so differently that you wouldn't believe he was the same person.

Later, they would lie in bed together and Thomas would share all the things he was too scared to speak of to anyone else. The man would listen as Thomas's hands flapped in time with his words. It would look calmer than anything you had seen in your life. It might look like happiness.

Of course, the view through the window wasn't very good, and it wasn't as if you were watching anyway. So you, like everyone else, would never know any of this. You would return to pick up your medicine and roll your eyes at the gruff man before you, the one who'd probably murdered a woman near identical to him. You'd whisper and judge, no matter how grateful you were that your maladies were so easily cured.

Your opinions would matter little to Thomas, as they always have. But in that nondescript alleyway, squished between a pub and cobbler, he would head upstairs, where the man is cooking dinner for them both, ready to listen to his partner's stories and waiting for his smile.

Love is a Haunting

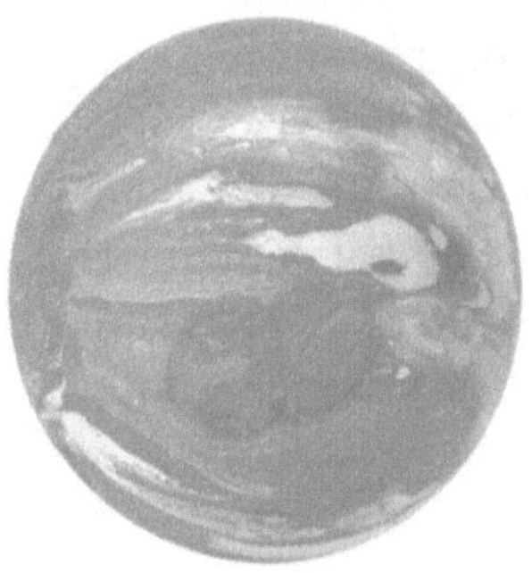

SYDNEY PAIGE GUERRERO

YOU ONCE TOLD me that ghosts are the world's way of remembering. I like the way it remembers you—your stoplight green nail polish and the butterfly clips in your hair, the Luzon-shaped birthmark on your knee and the crisp scent of your lemon shampoo. The way you frown when I curse, trying to hide your childish delight, and the way you light up when you finally summon enough ectoplasmic energy to pick up a pencil. Your joy is contagious. Especially when you make space for yourself, bit by bit.

I know you think that's not enough—that *you're* not enough for me, if not now, then someday. You're scared that I'll want more than a hand to hold, that I'll realize you're the only one bound to this house. You're scared I'll leave. But I want you to listen carefully from whatever corner of the house you're hiding in.

I like who I am when I'm with you. All I want is to hear about your favorite shows so we can find out how they ended. I want to laugh at the way you scrunch your nose up when I explain modern slang. I want to play you new songs that I think you'll like and find CDs of the bubblegum pop you miss. I want *you*.

And the truth is I have never felt love as a consequence of the body. Most days, my body is a stranger, and I have no more use for corporeality than you. I don't know what that makes me. Maybe I'm a memory in progress, and maybe *you* are the memory I'm trying to make. But I won't know if you don't come back, if you don't let me—let *us* try.

I don't understand how you think I could just *leave*. If you're staying, there's no moving on for me either. If you're bound to this house, then I'm bound to you. And, when my time comes, maybe I'll be able to linger here, where we can live in the light, like shadows do.

Don't you know there is more than one kind of haunting?

ᴘᴇᴘᴘᴇʀᴍɪɴᴛ ᴛᴇᴀ

Rᴀᴄʜᴇʟ Gᴜᴛɪɴ

S IMI HUDDLED IN their borrowed coat and tried not
to shiver as they reached for the stuffed roll their
housemate had set out for them. No matter how many
down coats and thick woolen sweaters Kari lent them, they
couldn't shake the chill from their bones. They ached to be
back home, where winter never got this cold.

But home meant Gran, and Gran was gone now. Had
it really been six weeks since she died?

At least the roll was fresh from the oven, blessedly hot.
The soft, spongy bread compressed between their teeth,
releasing a burst of rosemary and olive. The savory beef
filling warmed them from the inside out.

As they ate, they watched Kari flit around the kitchen,
murmuring to herself about this measurement or that
flavor. Kari had served Simi so many new foods, but it
was her *process* that fascinated them the most.

Culinary alchemy. That was what Kari called it. Mix a pinch of this with a dash of that, ingredients that bore only the vaguest resemblance to the desired outcome, one for each significant trait: color, texture, flavor. Kari made hot cocoa from stale breadcrumbs and brown sugar, or ground beef from mushrooms, cherries and oats.

And she was quick about it too. Five minutes of prep, then into the oven or frying pan it went. Back home, the same dishes would have taken hours.

Kari set out a row of glass prep bowls. "There's real mint this time," she said. "I found some at the market."

Simi stared intently at the wisps of steam curling up from inside their roll. "Okay."

"For the tea," Kari added, as if that weren't obvious.

"Sure."

Ever since Simi got the news six weeks ago, Kari had been trying to replicate Gran's tea. As if getting it just right might somehow heal the gaping wound in Simi's heart.

"Whole or crushed?" Kari asked.

"How should I know?" Simi had enjoyed Gran's tea countless times, but they'd never paid attention to how Gran made it. Not the way they paid attention when Kari cooked.

Kari sighed. "I really wish she'd written down the recipe."

"She never liked to make things easy." If she had, she wouldn't have been Gran. Simi dared to glance back up. "I wish you could've met her, though. She would've liked you."

Kari's pale cheeks flushed a vivid red. "Liked me enough to teach me how to make this tea?"

Simi barked out a single startled laugh. "As if."

"Well, let's try whole leaves this time." She lifted a shopping crate onto the counter. "No fresh ginger today. No lemons either. But I found some mandarins." She held up the bumpy orange fruit like a prize, then grabbed a microplane and started zesting. Next came a bulbous yellow root vegetable. Kari scraped at it with a peeler, and shavings tumbled into the bowl. And…was that brine she'd just opened?

"Color, acid, tang," Kari murmured as she sprinkled in the liquid. She grabbed a clean mixing wand from the holder by the sink and tapped it on the edge of the bowl three times, then started stirring. Her quiet murmur shifted into her usual wordless chant, and static prickled at the roots of Simi's hair.

Something *popped* as the spell coalesced, and Simi blinked. When they looked again, the bowl contained a heap of yellow powder, nearly as bright as Gran's finest lemons.

As Kari set to work on the ginger, anticipation squeezed at Simi's chest. Would this be the time she finally got it right? Was that even possible without fresh mint from the corner of Gran's garden? Without a lemon from the tree in the yard?

Was it possible to make Gran's tea without being *Gran*?

Still, Simi watched intently as Kari set a kettle on the stovetop and lined up two ceramic mugs on the counter to her right. She measured powder into each of them, then added a few mint leaves. The kettle whistled and she filled both mugs to the rim, then brought them to the table.

As Simi wrapped their hands around a mug, the familiar aroma caught them off-guard, enveloping them like one of Gran's giant hugs. Even so, they hesitated, not sure they could face the inevitable let-down when the flavor once again fell short.

But this was Kari sitting across from them. Kari, who always tried so hard.

They took a single cautious sip, and…

It was *home*.

The tea was Gran's kitchen, brewed and distilled into this plain white mug, and tears ran down their cheeks as they swallowed. Was it exactly right? No. But it was so very, *very* close. It was the freshness of the mint that Gran grew in her garden. The tartness of the lemons she picked from the yard.

It was Gran's arms, wrapped around them, squeezing too tightly. Gran's voice insisting that yes, they should leave home. "Go. You deserve a proper education." And never mind that Gran didn't tell them she was dying. Never mind that they couldn't make it back to say goodbye.

It was…

No.

It was just a cup of tea.

It was magic powder and a couple of mint leaves and it had no right to make them so upset.

They wiped their eyes on the sleeve of their borrowed jacket.

"Simi? What's wrong? Is it really that bad?"

"No. It's good. It's…just right." They forced down one more sip, as slow and deliberate as a careful goodbye, then pushed the mug away. "Please don't make it again."

Kari opened her mouth to speak, then changed her mind. She reached across the table to squeeze Simi's hand. "Want some hot cocoa instead?"

Simi nodded gratefully, and even managed a watery smile. "That sounds perfect."

They polished off the last of the stuffed roll, licking crumbs from their fingers as Kari grabbed a fresh wand and some scraps of stale bread. Soon enough, the smell of cocoa mingled with the peppermint and lemon, soothing away the last of their tears. Hot cocoa was *Kari's* drink, as much as tea was Gran's. It was a drink for *this* home, and as Simi breathed it in, they settled deeper into their seat, relaxing into the aroma's warm embrace.

THE SILENT SEA

ADA HOFFMANN

I CREPT DOWN THE rocky beach and watched the silent waves.

It had been three years since the sea stopped making a noise. I remembered what it had sounded like before: the crash of surf driven by the wind like a long, slow heart. The low static whoosh of it, lulling me half-asleep while I lay and watched the gulls. I'd liked those sounds, unlike the ones that remained to me now.

There was still plenty of sound on land. The honk and rumble of cars on streets, the blare of the television my housemates refused to turn off. Apartments and offices were still noisy: shouting, clanking, ringing little boxes. Where I could clench my eyes in concentration trying to type over the chatter, then be snapped at for every mistake. It was the sea, and only the sea, that had lost its voice.

The gulls' plaintive honk over the water was gone, though the gulls were not. A few of the white birds circled silently, taking turns to dip into the gray-blue water. One emerged holding a fish and the others dove in competitively while it wriggled in its captor's beak. A flurry of feathers blew out from the flock and floated across the waves. All silent, as if I was watching on a muted television. Someone had left an empty rowboat moored here, which bobbed in the water, not even creaking. It had been here for weeks, unwanted and untouched. I'd been watching.

Creeping closer, I put out a hand to the low gutters of water around the closest rocks. A small wave broke on its way to me, cascading down itself in a foamy veil. The water under my fingers rose up in response, reaching my knuckles, before the wave leached away again. I could smell the salt. My fingers ached with the sea's cold.

Back when the sea made a sound, there had been more people here, for good or ill. Waders and swimmers, despite the cold. Boats. Fishers and oil-riggers, humans grabbing what interested them in the thoughtless way that humans do; but also more beach-cleaners and conservationists, trying desperately to preserve what humans loved. Nobody really talked about the sea, these past three years, either to use it or to save it. Nobody went out in the water. As if the bustle of civilization was itself a sound.

They said that if you went far enough out in the waves, your own voice would stop up. Ships had been wrecked that way, I'd heard. But maybe it was just imagination. A few hundred feet back of me, where tall buildings rose up from the asphalt and cars jerked and honked in their long lines, there was sound aplenty. And that other sound, now that I'd been gone long enough. A yelling of my name. People behind me, urging me back to the land, back to my fruitless work. The sound and crush and urgency that I simply didn't want anymore.

Carefully, I climbed into the rowboat. I took hold of the oars. They were sturdy, solid things, polished smooth. Whoever abandoned this had cared for it once.

I pushed out into the waves and watched the scrambling shore-people shrink into the distance, still screaming, until at last their panicked noise fell away into the silence of the sea.

Omar's Perfect Falafel

RAMEZ YOAKEIM

OMAR'S SMALL STAND is set against the foundation of the Citadel's outer walls, its once vivid red and green paint faded into flaky pastels by a long succession of high noons. Stacks of flatbread compete for space with the cauldron at its heart, and the crescent of purple-rimmed enameled bowls that encircle it, each brimming with pickles, salads, and tahini. The other food stalls flaunt similar accoutrements to Omar's, but none could match his falafel: hand-formed spheres of apricot-sized pale green paste, smothered in sesame seeds right ahead of their baptismal plunge into boiling oil.

After a day of mind-numbing classes, I join the long queue—the line moves quickly and then there's Omar, perpetual toothy grin below his rampant mustache, eliciting reluctant echoes from even those who'd sworn off frivolity to survive their long and winding days. No one quite knows where Omar came from—some say he's Sa'idi, owing to the sun-drenched wheat of his skin and the drawl of his lilting speech. Others say he's a Jinn, wearing human flesh to lead the righteous astray. How else could he afford to charge so little? His competitors curse wherever he's from, wishing only he'd go back there. I don't care where he's from, though I rather like the idea of Omar the Jinn, here to take me elsewhere.

His grin grows a smidgen wider when he sees me, or so I convince myself. "Waleed, habibi, how was school today?" His voice booms yet remains intimate, his inquiry a confidence between friends.

"I'm studying at college, Omar," I say, helplessly grinning back at him. "I finished school years ago."

"We're always learning, habibi, about who we are and where we come from; about what makes us happy and what doesn't."

As he wraps the two bread halves overflowing with falafel in fresh newsprint, his eyes dim a little, and his head drops, after a sideways glance. I follow its trail to a wake of Council goons lurking in a web of whispers spun by Omar's competitors. He hands me the bundle, nods his chin at the conspirators and booms, "Let the people eat!"

†

THAT NIGHT, KNOWN unknowns trash his stand. Where it stood there's only a pile of debris now: splintered timber and shattered glass, chips of purple enamel lost in the dirt.

I tell myself I mean to ensure Omar's okay, as shadows grow shorter and I pace the gap between two tuk-tuks parked across a dusty lane from an old building's narrow front door. I tell myself many things, none of them the truth, as I'm caught between dreading and yearning, my heart at war with my head.

The impasse is broken when I glance up and see Omar in the narrow recessed doorway. "Waleed, is that you?"

I fill my eyes with him, more brazenly for all my angst, heart pounding, my extremities atremble. I know why

I'm here. Need burns through my skin with the merciless glare of the sky-cresting sun. Up close, the doorway seems so narrow and I wonder how Omar slips his muscular bulk through it every day. Does he graze its edges? Does it rattle at his touch?

He waits inside, smiling, not the marketplace fixture of swagger and challenge, but a softer one, warmer, knowing, inviting. "I thought it was you," Omar says, leaning against a helical staircase that rose towards the sky. My tongue vanishes, deserting me, as has my breath, stolen by the blood thundering through my veins. It doesn't matter, I nod.

"Come." Omar grabs my hand and guides me into the darkness underneath the stairs.

†

His room is not at all what I expected.

I half-wondered if it'd be the gateway to some marvelous Jinn palace. The other half dreaded the reality of a musty and dank cavity, like the sort I shared with two other students. Forgotten nooks under stairs or atop roofs, buttressing the airy, balconied apartments of those of better means.

The reality lies somewhere in between. Omar's room is clean and the only scents are lingering hints of citrus and cinnamon. Half the room is devoted to knee-high earthenware urns overflowing with soaking fava beans, alongside an ancient stone grinder. I look for sacks of dried beans but find none. The room's other half holds a neatly made bed covered by a black-and-white wool blanket, a chipped Formica-topped table, and a squat metal-girded chest.

A well forms where Omar sits on the bed. He pats a spot next to him. There's nowhere else in the room to sit, except maybe the tiled floor. "Tell me why you came."

"I wanted to l-learn how you make your falafel," I stammer until I make the mistake of looking into his eyes. I lose my balance and fall into his well.

He steadies me, wrapping his arm around my shoulder. "Are you sure?"

I know what he's asking. I rest my palm on his chest and nod.

Up close, Omar smells earthy and wholesome, like fresh cilantro and tomato vines, and when he pulls off his shirt his brown hairy chest glows with a sheen like falafels fresh from the oil. In the whirlwind of skin meeting skin that follows, I uncover new universes in the intervals between pleasured gasps and guttural moans. When it feels like we're flying, I open my eyes to find that we are. We tumble in the air, my weight supported by Omar's, our limbs entwined, his body shining with dawn's first light.

"You *are* Jinn!" I exclaim, too engrossed to be scared of falling.

"A migrant in your realm." Omar's laugh is a deep rumble that travels through our connected bodies. "All I want is to sate the hungry."

I start to say that I'll always hunger for tenderness, for safety, for joy. Hunger for him, his touch, his scent, his grin. But too many yearnings jostle within. In the end, I only say, "I know."

†

LATER, I WAKE up to garlic and cumin and frying falafel. I peek through slitted eyes to find Omar standing by a small butane burner below a dusty, wall-mounted ventilation fan, his features shimmying and swaying in the haze of boiling oil.

"You shouldn't do that nude," I say, my eyes at last unashamed. "Splattering oil is sure to hurt like hell, even if you're Jinn."

He looks at me and grins. In a moment, the burner is off and he's by my side, a still-steaming bowl in one hand. "I wanted you to have something to eat to start the day." I didn't realize how long we spent in the windowless room.

I take a bite of the still hot falafel and close my eyes, lost in bliss, until I feel his finger tracing a path along my legs. I shudder and set aside any lingering fears—of who might find out and what they might do—and lap the moment's promise, refusing to soil it with what ifs. My chest rumbles with unfamiliar contentment.

Omar draws me closer. His touch sends goosebumps racing across my skin. "Is that for the falafel or for me?" he asks through his mustachioed grin, and my lips, meeting his, answer him.

My heart thumps and my breath heaves ragged as we kiss. A lifetime of yearnings finds release. In the shadow of the Citadel's walls, aren't I as much a foreigner as Omar is? Both of us desperate to belong, to connect, to cling onto every scrap of long-denied joy that blows our way.

I wrap my arms around him and let go.

The Hour Between Yesterday and Tomorrow

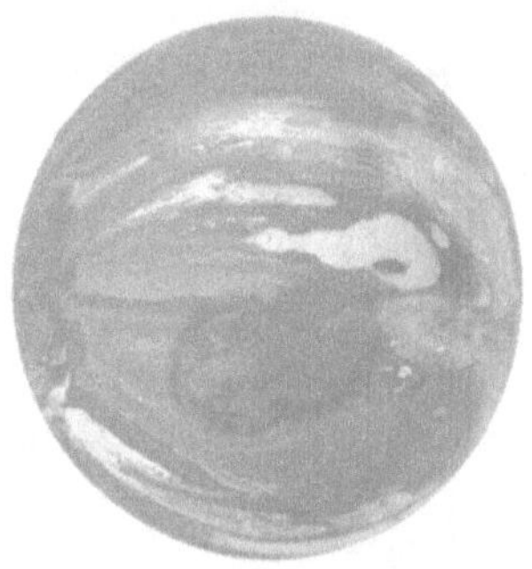

MICHELLE EXLER

00:00. After a long and tiring day, all the hands on the watch come to a halt when they reach twelve. Sisyphus has, impossibly, reached the goal. Gets to rest. You're watching like a hawk, just in case it's all a lie, but no. Time has stopped. You snicker because it still feels more normal than everything else that's happened.

00:00. How will you know it's been an hour?

00:00. Your palms are clammy. The unknowing gives you anxiety. You look up, finally. The harsh LEDs greet you without remorse. The gas station is empty—well, empty of anybody but you. Should you steal a chocolate bar or a pack of chewing gum? Should you go to the restroom and deliberately not pay fifty cents? Should you jump over the counter to steal fifty cents? Or should you sit on your hands and wait? Is it even waiting if there's no time?

00:00. She walks in. You would be reminded of everything she is or isn't if you weren't so aware of it already; if it wasn't pressed into you by her own hands; if you didn't recognize her as a part of you wherever. Whenever.

"I thought this place was abandoned," she says upon entering.

00:00. "It's abandoned all the time except for the hour between yesterday and tomorrow."

00:00. Raindrops pitter-patter on the tall glass windows. She's wearing your skirt, by the way, did you notice that? Yes, you must have. She stole it the first time she visited your old room in your parents' house. While you were busy talking about the posters still hanging above your bed (so, while you were talking about how you loved all these women but you didn't know you loved women), she rummaged through your drawers. She wanted to see the real you, she said. Was the real you the lace on your underwear or the handcuffs under your bed or the dirty pantyhose you forgot to wash? She never told you, but she did steal the skirt. She wears it still.

00:00. "Betty, why are we here?"

00:00. This is, indeed, a timeless question. It deserves a timeless answer.

00:00. "I don't know," you whisper.

00:00. You are here to commemorate. Here's to the fights you lost and she won and you won and she lost. Here's to the eye bags that you conceal from everybody but her. Here's to the shitty coffee she makes and you drink with a thank you. Here's to the purple lipstick called Belle Of The Ball that you both wore so you could kiss at her parents' Christmas party and nobody would know. Here's to the ring pop you bought last summer—an intended joke you never carried out and ate by yourself in the backseat of your car. Here's to her food poisoning, when you held her hair as she retched and retched and retched. Here's to the hand-holding, shared dinners, grocery lists, gasbills, insidejokes, kissesfightsroadtripspresentslovenotesfartsconfessions. It's a neverending road, this.

00:00. Wait, are you here to be angry? Here's to the naked ass of that woman you saw driving right into your wife on that sunny afternoon last week when you got home early. Surprise! Here's to her!

00:00. "I still love you," you say because it's okay to utter such things when time stands still for an hour in a neon-lit gas station.

00:00. "I love you too, Betty."

00:00. "Goodbye now?"

00:00. She nods. You take her in one last time. Under these lights, she doesn't look beautiful. She looks gaunt and sickly. Her contour seems to be cutting her face wide open. The skirt always fit you better. You would still choose her, which is okay in some ways, but you would still die for her, and that's far from. It's time to turn the lights off.

00:01.

THREE DEATHS, ONE GRAVE

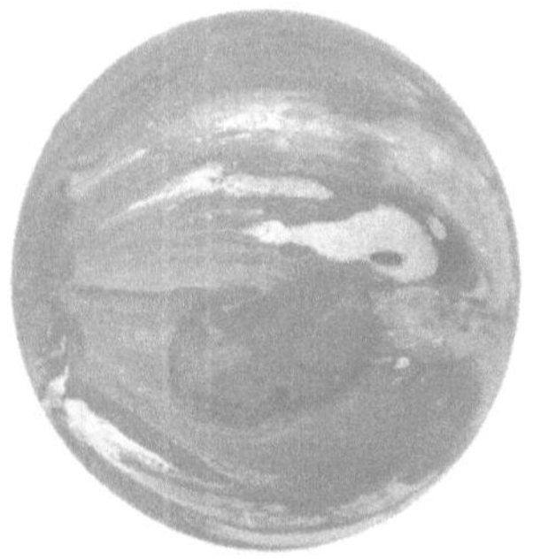

HANNA A. NIRAV

0. Grief

IN YOUR ABSENCE, my world has become empty.

The rooms are too big, our bed too cold. The koel visits every morning but its call comes from oceans away. Food turns to dust on my tongue. Every second stretches longer than the last as life spins around me, a monochrome mockery of what it should have been.

My skin aches for you. My eyes seek you in every corner. My mouth misses the shape of your smile.

I miss you, my love. We had so little time together.

†

HERE IS THE spell I have devised:

1. A piece of you.

BEGINNING IS ALWAYS the most difficult step. The inertia of not-doing is as bad as a habit, and equally as difficult to overcome—but the thought of you spurs me forward, inch by inch.

And so I crawl towards the earth behind our home. Just beneath the rambutan tree, the ground still brown where it was recently disturbed, a stark contrast against the grass around it.

Did you know the earth abandoned me? 35 years I lived with her whispering along to my every thought, and yet, in losing you, I lost her as well. And what use is a death witch who cannot hear her magic?

In one grave, I buried three deaths.

Now, it is time to desecrate all three of us.

I kneel by the mound of your final resting place, and the ground is hard and cold against my fingers. This last bed I moulded for you, I now unmake.

When I find your skull deep in the earth, I cradle it close and kiss it. Soon, I will kiss you again.

2. Blood, a gift.

HAVING BEGUN, IT is easier to keep going. Like a rock tipped over the cliff, I, too, gain fervour with motion.

It is a jarring sight, but the village is as lively as it has always been. An injustice. All the world should mourn you as I have, but these people have the audacity to carry on with their lives, blissed and blessed.

No matter.

For you, I choose a young diver, the eldest of a family of orphans. The knife glints, moonlight catching along its smooth edge, and she bleeds red against the white of your cheeks, the ivory of your still-perfect teeth.

Where one life ends, another will resume.

3. A piece of me.

DURING MY TIME with you, I grew negligent. The earth is a jealous master, and she marked me as one of hers from the moment I drew my first breath.

But you, my love, claimed me as well.

When our eyes met, you claimed me. Every laugh you drew from me, every smile you gifted me—every moment we spent together, you staked your claim to me. You made me your wife, and you, mine.

My devotion to you far outweighed what I gave the earth. It is shameful to pretend I do not know why she abandoned me.

I must make amends. The same knife I used to bleed that girl, I now turn onto myself.

More than anything, I wish to see you again.

And so to the earth, my eternal master, I gift my eyes.

The pain is like a vacuum; all at once, everything recedes, as if what little is left in my life is drawing back like the ocean before a tsunami, except that final wave never comes. If I had thought it too quiet before, this new, deeper silence is all-consuming.

But then, there she is, waiting, ready to share once more her secrets. When I reach out, the earth meets me halfway, wrapping itself around my mind, tightening against my heart and throat. The earth holds everything—the skittering ants, the crawling worms. The whispered cries of the unjustly dead, the whimpers of the tortured. Everything is familiar—yet not, and a sense of unease begins to spread beneath my skin even as I smile, even as I weep because most importantly,

It holds you.

4. Longing.

IN THIS NEW silence, everything waits. The koel watches from nearby, perched on a tree by the house.

Half-buried in the earth and in you, I am empty-eyed and open-mouthed. I wait.

Half-buried in the earth, you are inching your way out, slowly, soundlessly, bit by agonizing bit.

The earth has me frozen in her grip, but I am not going anywhere. Oh, to witness this moment I have longed for, even by proxy—nothing could possibly compare to the joy of being here as the earth embraces you for me, wrapping around your bare bones like a second skin, nestling close between ribs and neck and teeth. My heart soars and my lungs swell as it opens your mouth to say:

"My love,

I've missed you."

Contributors

Brie Atienza is a Filipino-Indonesian writer who lives in Singapore. Her short fiction has previously appeared in *Constelación* and *Ombak*. She's worked on *Vynestra*, a 5e campaign setting based on the Roman Republic. You can find her @thesharkwrites on Twitter.

Malik Berry is a writer and community organizer based in Baltimore, MD. Their work includes fiction, theatre, and poetry, and has appeared in Expat Press, *Meow Meow Pow Pow*, *World Hunger*, *DON'T SUBMIT*, *Across the Margin*, and *God's Cruel Joke*. They get inspiration from performing mutual aid and fostering relationships with attractive video game characters. They can be reached on Instagram (@malikb_jpg) and Bluesky (@malikbtxt.bsky.social).

Devon Borkowski is a writer, artist, and actor from the Rappahannock tribe of Virginia. She was raised in the New Jersey Pine Barrens, and graduated from Rutgers New Brunswick with a BFA in Visual Arts class of 2022. Her poetry and short stories have appeared in *The Dillydoun Review*, *The Closed Eye Open*, and *Room Magazine*.

Celia Daniels likes to toe the line between fantasy and reality by making her damsels, rogues, and knights contend with the complexity of smartphones (or at least the printing press). She hails from Indiana and alternates between spending time with her cat, Achilles, and tap, tap, tapping away on her computer. You can find her work in *Timeless Tales*, *The Molotov Cocktail*, and F(r)iction's "Dually Noted."

Michelle Exler is as much a reader as she is a writer. If she's not reading whichever queer books she can get her hands on, she's writing anything queer she can think of; if she's not doing either, she's reminiscing about her film school years or watching movies, which makes her reminisce. She's a living breathing example of the circle of life, as we all are. She lives in a small European country with her girlfriend, a dog, and a cat.

Tessa Fisher is a trans lesbian SFF writer and astrobiologist at the University of Ariona's Steward Observatory. When she's not doing science or writing, her hobbies include burlesque dancing, running, and singing in the Phoenix Women's Chorus. Her work has appeared in *Analog, Fireside,* and *Translunar Travelers Lounge,* as well as multiple anthologies. She currently resides in Phoenix with her wife, a vocal rescue cat, and an aloof bearded dragon. For more info, check out her website at tessafisher.com, or follow her at tessafisher.bsky.social.

Sydney Paige Guerrero is a Filipino speculative fiction writer and scholar with a soft spot for the weird and whimsical. Her work has appeared in *Fantasy Magazine, Cast of Wonders, Apex Magazine, Tales and Feathers Magazine, Fusion Fragment* and other venues. You can find out more about her at www.sydneypaigeguerrero.wordpress.com.

Rachel Gutin is a writer and special education teacher. Her short fiction has appeared in a number of publications including *Escape Pod, Cast of Wonders,* and *Small Wonders.* She lives in Brooklyn, NY, and is a member of the organizing team for Brooklyn Speculative Fiction Writers. You can find her online at rachelgutin.wordpress.com.

Anja Hendrikse Liu (she/they) writes stories of magics and futures. Their work has appeared in *Uncharted, Diabolical Plots, We're Here: The Best Queer Speculative Fiction 2022,* and elsewhere. They have a master's in Narrative Futures, a day job at an outdoors nonprofit, and a penchant for unusual baked goods. Find Anja online at anjahl.com/author.

Ada Hoffmann is the author of the OUTSIDE space opera trilogy, as well as dozens of speculative short stories and poems. Ada's work has been a finalist for the Philip K. Dick Award, the Compton Crook Award, and the WSFA Small Press Award, among others. They are also the author of the Autistic Book Party review series, devoted to in-depth #ownvoices discussions of autism representation in speculative fiction. Ada is an adjunct professor of computer science, as well as a former semi-professional soprano, tabletop gaming enthusiast, and LARPer. They live in eastern Ontario.

Morris Hinkle (they/them) is a queer trans author currently attending veterinary school in the Midwest. Their stories have previously appeared in *Reckoning.*

Ash Howell (they/them) is a speculative fiction writer living on the shores of Lake Michigan. Their work has appeared in *Lightspeed, Baffling Magazine, Astrolabe,* and elsewhere. They are a 2023 alum of Viable Paradise, a software engineer, and parent of two voracious bookworms.

Lindsay King-Miller is the author of *Ask a Queer Chick: A Guide to Sex, Love, and Life for Girls who Dig Girls* (Plume, 2016). Her debut novel, *The Z Word,* was published by Quirk Books. She lives in Denver, CO with her partner and their two children.

D.K. Lawhorn (he/him) is a citizen of the Monacan Indian Nation and lives on his ancestral land in Virginia with his legion of rescue cats. His stories have appeared in *ANMLY, khōréō magazine, HAD,* and *The Massachusetts Review.* He was part of the Tin House Fall Workshop '22 and Clarion West '23. He is a graduate of Randolph College's MFA in Creative Writing program where he concentrated his studies on Native American speculative fiction. Follow him on Twitter @d_k_lawhorn or visit his website at dklawhorn.com.

P. H. Low is a Locus-, Ignyte-, and Rhysling-nominated Malaysian American writer and poet whose debut novel, *These Deathless Shores,* was published by Orbit Books (US) and Angry Robot (UK). Their shorter work can be found in *Strange Horizons, Fantasy Magazine, Reactor,* and *Diabolical Plots,* among others. P. H. has a bad habit of moving cities every few years, but can be found online at ph-low.com.

Avra Margariti is a queer author and Pushcart-nominated poet with a fondness for the dark and the darling. Avra's work haunts publications such as *Vastarien, Asimov's, Strange Horizons, F&SF, The Deadlands, Lackington's,* and *Reckoning.* Avra lives and studies in Athens, Greece. You can find Avra on twitter (@avramargariti).

Sam J. Miller's books have been called "must-reads" and "bests of the year" by *NPR, Entertainment Weekly, USA Today,* and *O: The Oprah Magazine,* among others. They've also been banned in Florida, and stolen by AI. His short fiction has been published in places like *The Kenyon Review, Vogue Italia, Tor.com,* Asimov's, and more. He's received the Nebula, Locus, and Shirley Jackson Awards. He's also the last in a long line of butchers. Sam lives in New York City, and at <u>samjmiller.com</u>

Kengo Nelson is a romance writer and desert cactus transplanted to New England. He contributes to Kansai-themed literary zine Kyoto Cryptids, and can be found posting infrequently on Bluesky @kengonelson.

Hanna A. Nirav is a writer who has been telling stories all her life. She is an avid reader, hardcore casual gamer and loves food. As a Malay-Indian Malaysian, she is no longer interested in toeing the line between intersecting circles. You can find her on Twitter @hanstilltweets or on Bluesky @hanstillhere. Her short fiction has been published in collections by Neon Hemlock Press and *Speculatively Queer*, and you can check out her other work at hanmuses.wordpress.com.

Jared Povanda is a writer, poet, and freelance editor from the Finger Lakes region of New York, as well as the co-founder and co-EIC of the literary journal Bulb Culture Collective. He has been nominated twice for the Pushcart Prize, multiple times for Best of the Net and Best Microfiction, and his fiction has been shortlisted for the Bridport Prize. His story "Missing Pieces" was highlighted as a Must-Read Speculative Short Fiction pick at *Reactor Magazine* (formerly Tor) in 2022. You can find more of his work in numerous literary journals including *Wigleaf, Phoebe Journal,* and *Passages North.*

Matt Richardson (they/he) is a queer fiction author and editor from Australia, whose stories experiment with points of view and the lives of queer characters. They are the former lead editor for *Meridian Australis* and *Swine Magazine.* Their previous works can be found in *Apparition Literary Magazine, TL;DR Press* charity anthologies, and *Swine Magazine.*

Erin Rockfort (they/she) is a queer, neurodivergent writer and therapist based in Ottawa, Ontario. Their work often explores topics of personhood, connection, and expectation. She has been published by *Translunar Travelers Lounge* and Renaissance Press, and is an organizer for the SFFH conference Can*Con. They can be found @ pineapplefury for aggrieved thoughts on romantasy.

Sydney Sackett (she/her) is a Frostburg State University grad who currently edits full-time, and pursues prose and 4X space games on the side. Some of her work appears in *Etherea, Menacing Hedge, Allegory,* and *Not One of Us.* She can be tracked down to sydneybsackett.wixsite.com/website.

A.D. Sui is a Ukrainian-born, internationally raised speculative writer, Nebula winner, and Aurora, and Theodore Sturgeon Memorial Award finalist. They are the author of *The Dragonfly Gambit* (2024), *The Iron Garden Sutra* (2026), and more than two dozen short stories. A failed academic and retired fencer, they spend most days wrangling their two dogs and tending to their myriads of tropical plants. You can find them on most social media platforms as @thesuiway.

Elena Sichrovsky (she/they/it) is a queer disabled Austrian-Taiwanese writer. Their work explores themes of identity, trauma, and grief through the lens of body horror. Its stories have been published with *Radon, Nightmare, Cosmic Horror Monthly, Titan Books,* and *Tenebrous Press,* among others. Read more at www.elenasichrovsky.com.

Simo Srinivas' stories have appeared in several speculative fiction magazines and anthologies, including *Fantasy Magazine, Strange Horizons, khōréō,* and *Archive of the Odd,* among others. Simo was a 2025 Lambda Literary Fellow and Tenebrous Press' Brave New Weird Breakout Author of 2023. Find them online at srinivassimo.com.

Leon Tomova is a first-generation Slavic immigrant based in Germany. When not working on their PhD thesis, they write stories about queer mayhem and triumph. In their time away from the keyboard, you can catch them at the gym, dancing, or sipping an iced oat milk latte. Find them on Bluesky @leont.bsky.social.

A one-time engineer and educator, **Ramez Yoakeim** writes mostly about outsiders finding hope in dire circumstances, including "Rise Again" and "More Than Trinkets," selected for Tor.com's Must-Read Speculative Short Fiction. You'll find his stories in Flame Tree Press and Erewhon Books anthologies, podcasts from *Cast of Wonders* and *StarShipSofa*, and online in *Translunar Travelers Lounge, UtopiaSF, Sci Phi Journal,* and *Aurealis*, among others. Discover more on his website, yoakeim.com.

Catherine Yu writes dark speculative fiction. She was born in Nanjing and is now based in New York. She is the author of *Direwood, Helga,* and *The Devil's in the Dancers*. Her short fiction has appeared in *Fantasy* and the *Death in the Mouth* anthology.

Liza Wemakor is a writer and a Ph.D. candidate in UC Riverside's English Department. She writes and studies speculative fiction and Black American literature. Her fiction is published in *Strange Horizons, Anathema Magazine, Fiyah, Baffling Magazine,* and elsewhere. She is a member of the 2023 Clarion West Writers' Workshop cohort. Her novella *Loving Safoa* was published in 2023.

Bree Wernicke is an actor and speculative fiction writer from Los Angeles. Her work has been nominated for the Rhysling Award and appeared in *Strange Horizons, Baffling Magazine, Haven Spec, Fusion Fragment,* and more. Her website is breewernicke.com

NEW EDGE SWORD & SORCERY MAGAZINE

Made with love for the classics and an inclusive, boundary-pushing approach to storytelling!

Fiction & Non-Fiction
Digital, Softcover, and Hardcover
www.newedgeswordandsorcery.com

About Baffling

Baffling Magazine is a quarterly online magazine of flash fiction that publishes fantasy, science fiction & horror stories with a queer bent. Stories are first shared online with our patrons throughout the year. If you'd like to support us, please visit patreon.com/neonhemlock.

Visit us online at www.bafflingmag.com.

About the Press

Neon Hemlock is a Washington, DC-based small press publishing speculative fiction, rad zines, and queer chapbooks. Publishers Weekly once called us "the apex of queer speculative fiction publishing" and we're still beaming. Learn more about us at neonhemlock.com and on social medias at @neonhemlock.

www.ingramcontent.com/pod-product-compliance
Lightning Source LLC
Chambersburg PA
CBHW031543310726
48971CB00008B/2606